Broken Eye Books is an independent press, here to bring you the odd, strange, and offbeat side of speculative fiction. Our stories tend to blend genres, highlighting the weird and blurring its boundaries with horror, sci-fi, and fantasy.

Support weird. Support indie.

brokeneyebooks.com
facebook.com/brokeneyebooks
instagram.com/brokeneyebooks

—praise for author—
THE MOSQUITO FLEET

"Sense of wonder meets sense of the Weird in this compelling and original space opera. I loved it!" (**John Joseph Adams**, series editor of *Best American Science Fiction and Fantasy* and Hugo Award-winning editor of *Lightspeed Magazine*)

"*The Mosquito Fleet* is great science fiction with a Lovecraftian twist. The worlds and technology are strange, but the characters are people we understand completely and care about. The action comes hot and heavy yet leaves space for emotional moments." (**Daryl Gregory**, award-winning author of *Spoonbenders*)

"In Andrew Penn Romine's *The Mosquito Fleet*, organic technologies are used not only to create sentient starships, but synthetic beings perhaps more human than their masters, as embodied in our complex protagonist, Lira. Filled with fast-paced action, intriguing characters, vivid imagery, and more than a dash of cosmic horror, *The Mosquito Fleet* is a warp jump into a scintillatingly imaginative future." (**Jeffrey Thomas**, author of the Punktown series.)

"Andy Romine's *The Mosquito Fleet* is the warp-driven, wide-ranging, and biotically well-oiled adventure you've been waiting for! With an eye for kinetic action anchored in the (mostly) human hearts of these gripping characters, *The Mosquito Fleet* is an expertly navigated jaunt through interstellar sci-fi, splatastically fungal body horror, and philosophical hyperjumps of the most entertaining kind." (**Gordon B. White**, Shirley Jackson Award and Brad Stoker Award finalist)

—OTHER STORIES—

"Romine deftly weaves a story that deals with guilt and regret and memory—specifically the gradual deterioration of memory and the utter confusion that causes for the person it is happening to." (**Maria Haskins**, reviewing "Miles and Miles and Miles" for *B&N Reads*)

The Mosquito Fleet

THE MOSQUITO FLEET by ANDREW PENN ROMINE

Published by
Broken Eye Books
www.brokeneyebooks.com

All rights reserved.
Copyright © 2024 Broken Eye Books and the author.
Cover illustration by Tithi Luadthong.
Cover design by Tithi Luadthong and Scott Gable.
Interior design by Scott Gable.
Editing by Scott Gable and C. Dombrowski.
Photography by Jenn Reese.

978-1-940372-77-8 (trade paperback)
978-1-940372-84-6 (hardcover)

All characters and events in this book are fictional.
Any resemblance to persons living or dead is coincidental.

The Mosquito Fleet

ANDREW PENN ROMINE

To Mom, who taught me that scary can be fun.

PART 1: THE STARS, HOW DIFFERENT FROM NIGHT TO NIGHT

Five seconds after the biotic ferry *Grass is Greener* shunts out of warp space, Lira notices the stars are different—not where they ought to be.

An amber dot hums into existence on the navigator's holochart and stays there: *Navigational Hazard, Class V.*

An error, surely.

Lira drums the curved screen, an indisputable human habit, but the stubborn dot remains. No error. The hazard spews gravitational waves, though the mass registers less than that of one of the enormous grain barges on the long boost out of Crockett's Star.

No error. A miscalculation.

Lira's synthetic muscles tighten across her chest in approximation of another human response. Anxiety. The last time she miscalculated a jump, a lot of people died.

"Skipper," she calls over her shoulder, peering past the corner of the acceleration couch. Captain Erinn Juarez yawns in her aft command console, removing her hypersleep cuff and rubbing her wrist where the soporific electrodes had been attached. Her eyes are fuzzy with hypersleep, but worry lines carve deep furrows in her aging face at the alarm in Lira's tone.

"Nav hazard dead ahead. Class five." Lira says, omitting for the moment that they're off course as well. "Five-zero two-three-one kilometers." The navigator suppresses a tremor in her left hand. That's how it always begins. Headaches follow and then the stimbulb. The sting in the crook of her arm and then the release.

"You sure, Lira? I don't see anything," says Pete Driscoll, the quartermaster seated at the helm station forward of her. Driscoll had piloted *Grass is Greener* for almost ten years before Juarez purchased the charter and with her captaincy brought Lira onboard. He'd logged no less than three official protests at being passed up for chief mate.

Driscoll leans over his helm console, looking out through the trapezoidal viewports of the galley-like bridge in an exaggerated show. Nothing but the black of deep space beyond. He throws a grin back at Lira, but his eyes don't contain his smile.

"Are you defective? Look at my chart," she snaps at him, shocked at her own defensiveness. Driscoll's jaw drops in astonishment.

"Lira?" Worry mounts in Juarez's brow.

Such combative outbursts are rare. Lira flushes with embarrassment. "Apologies, Skipper, Driscoll," Lira replies, "but *Grass is Greener* doesn't lie."

"Give me a visual," Juarez orders.

Lira nods, thumbing the ship's astronomical cameras toward the hazard. A blurry holo appears on the viewport, showing a dark, pear-shaped patch of deep space against a darker, starless backdrop. The patch is shrouded with hazy, pale gases. The amber lines of the ferry's projected course plunge into the heart of the hazard.

Lira's chest tightens. This scenario recalls too much of what happened at asteroid Adamson A621 aboard the *Highline*. Two such egregious jump calculations in one's career are highly improbable. She tries to keep her own brow from furrowing.

"All stop," the captain orders Driscoll.

As the ferry rumbles in response, Lira adjusts its sensors. It's an antiquated system with low resolution, mostly mechanical antenna that were favored in an earlier era of shipbuilding. Juarez would have been wise to upgrade to full organic sensor vanes years ago, but the margins are thin in the ferry business.

Like Lira, *Grass is Greener* is a biotic construct, a blend of semi-organic and mechanical components. The ship's steel hull, laid over a century before, protects the crew against the exceptional rigors of spaceflight. Deep within that reinforced shell, however, its biotic core instinctively translates the shifting realities of warp space into hard navigational data. Synthetics, developed from the same science that created biotic ships, serve as a bridge between the crew and the animal intelligence of their ship.

"Saints of shit. What is that?" Driscoll mutters.

Lira suppresses another tremor. The first sullen pangs of headache trace the seams of her skull.

Stress is an unacceptable response, she reprimands herself. *The crew is counting on you.*

"Skipper," she confesses. "We're off course." The headache intensifies. She'll need her injections soon.

"You think?"

"We arrived at Crockett's Star," Lira assures her. "But we're at the heliopause, far short of our arrival coordinates."

Captain Juarez gives Lira a look freighted with their shared history.

"Can we chart around that thing?" Juarez winces, toying with the hypersleep cuff. "And just shunt back to warp?"

The skipper closes her eyes and runs a hand through the mop of her short, gray hair. She emits a heavy sigh. Juarez was diagnosed with liver cancer last year, and despite a series of expensive organ replacements, both artificial and biotic, she's only getting sicker. She can't afford treatments, and she can't afford retirement. Lira wonders what happens when Juarez dies. Will Lira's role in the *Highline* disaster remain secret? Pondering the question now only makes the cracks in Lira's head grow wider.

"The object's emitting gravitational waves consistent with artificial gravity, but I believe we can skirt around it without incident."

"'Without incident?'" mocks Driscoll. "We just came out of warp and ran into the only object for millions of miles around. What do you call that?"

"Improbable," Lira agrees, troubled.

"So what the hell is it?" Juarez asks.

Lira reads the sensor data. On the holo, faint outlines of a wide tail stretch for a million kilometers behind the hazard. Save for the unusual gravitational readings, it could be a long-period or hyperbolic comet, albeit one that's not on any of their charts.

"A comet perhaps," she says doubtfully, "Approximately thirty-five kilometers in diameter. *Grass is Greener* detects some outgassing. Methane, ammonia, even some oxygen."

"Any debris?"

"A handful of smaller bodies in loose orbit around the nucleus, but the data are inconclusive."

"How the hell did this happen, Lira?"

Lira flushes at the accusation implicit in the skipper's question. The *history*. She can't look Driscoll in the eye when he turns to face her.

"Perhaps I made an error interpreting *Grass is Greener*'s warp space calculations," she admits.

Juarez grunts, and Lira can almost hear her saying, "That's twice."

"Saints of shit, we'll be late getting into Crockett no matter what," Juarez mutters. Driscoll shakes his head and reaches for his headset.

Lira doesn't understand why *Grass is Greener* would give her the wrong jump information. The ship navigated warp space by instinct, not conscious thought. There's no possibility for error or deception.

Unlike with a synthetic.

Lira isn't lying though, so it means the error belongs to her.

"Skipper, I offer to relieve myself of duty," Lira proposes. It's the only solution certain to prevent her from making further errors.

"Like hell," Juarez snorts. "I need you to chart us around that thing. Then calculate a new jump. Otherwise, it'll be weeks before we cruise home."

Lira spends several minutes plotting a new course that takes them around the comet. Juarez orders Driscoll to follow it. The dark blot of the navigational hazard heaves well to the side. Lira breathes a sigh of relief. New warp coordinates will take longer.

Driscoll yelps and tears his comm-phones from his head. An ear-piercing squawk shrills from the speakers and ebbs to a low warble.

"I was trying to raise Crockett control, and that's what I got," he says, rubbing his ears. He puts the signal on speaker. Mostly they hear the normal click of background radiation, but the warble remains like low-throated birdsong.

"Might be the comet's gravitational waves," Lira says, though she's far from sure that it's actually a comet. What else might it be though? Lira leans back from her console, irritated with herself. Synthetics aren't supposed to be susceptible to this sort of self-indulgent brooding. Perhaps the faults in her navigational core have spread to her emotional nodes. She'll ask Abe to check later.

As if reading her thoughts, the skipper seeks Abe's advice first, summoning him up on the comm.

"Heya, Skipper," the cheerful, baritone voice of the chief biotic engineer replies.

Abram Mistri is the longest serving crew member aboard *Grass is Greener*. Unlike Driscoll, he's never once jockeyed for command. Abe's content to live in the warren of biomass conduits and drive machineries of the engineering deck. He's got an easy touch with biotic systems; Lira should know. He loves his ship almost as much as he loves its navigator.

The bunk, narrow and cramped. Abe's rough-shaven cheeks brushing against her thighs . . .

More self-indulgence. Lira tries and fails to focus on her navigational calculations.

"Mistri," Juarez says, "we've shunted from warp space early, on course for what looks to be a rogue comet. Lira's charted us around it for now, but I'm worried about making another jump with respect to debris."

"Hmm. That's tricky."

Lira knows Abe well enough to read the concern echoed in his truncated reply. He'll be scratching that bald, brown dome of his with a nimble finger and worrying about the ferry's hull. He converses in muffled tones with his co-engineer, Magnus Lin. Lin looks after the mechanical innards of the ship with the same care Abe pays the biotic ones.

"Skipper," Abe says, "do what you gotta. Mags and I are confident the hull can take it. We've weathered rough seas before."

"We start plowing through debris, Skipper," Driscoll warns, "the passengers are going to full-on panic."

Juarez closes her eyes. The shallowness of her breathing indicates probable discomfort from her illness.

"Skipper," Lira suggests, "I'll go down to the main sensor compartment and calibrate for hazardous debris."

She could also stop by the infirmary on her way and get painkillers for Juarez. Stimbulbs for herself.

The skipper cuts her a pained look with a raised eyebrow to let Lira know she's onto her scheme.

"Do it," she relents with a grimace. "And Abe, are you still listening?"

"Aye, Skipper," the engineer answers.

"Meet Lira there. If you can coax some performance from the sensory fronds, I'll feel better." *And keep an eye on my navigator too,* is the unspoken command.

Lira and Abe's relationship isn't a secret among the small crew, but Driscoll snickers all the same.

"Just don't coax anything else," he mumbles.

The skipper clenches her teeth through a wave of pain, "What are you, *five,* Pete?"

Chastened but still giggling, Driscoll goes back to his comm board, trying to raise Crockett's Star. Lira stands from her station and heads toward the exit hatch.

"What about the passengers?" she asks the captain.

Juarez grabs the hand-mic for the PA.

"I'll announce there's been a delay. If any of the kiddos happen to corner you, tell them the same thing. Got it?"

The "kiddos" are the ferry's deckhands, a trio of young apprentices working on an internship. Gregarious and mostly reliable, they love gossip and are a bit too chummy with the passengers. Juarez likes cheap, good-looking labor, but the truth is, they work efficiently, and she's been considering making an offer to hire at least one of them full-time. Lira approves.

"I won't say a thing," Lira says.

Juarez gives her another odd look. Lira's promise echoes the very words the skipper said to her ten years past in the aftermath of Adamson A621 and the destruction of the *Highline.*

The haunted look on the skipper's pallid and sweat-sheened face lingers in Lira's mind long after she leaves the bridge.

Durance Pike wipes the hypersleep from his eyes, hardly believing the sight that fills his porthole.

A thrill rises as he presses his face to the window. His tattered seat rumbles as the ferry slows, and his hypersleep cuff rolls unsecured from the armrest. Electricity tingles at the end of his fingers. The thin line of Pike's lips, long unaccustomed to variations in their stony geometry, flexes upward in a grin.

A comet: a faint but unmistakable shadow tumbling against the deeper black of space, rises into the ferry's path like a dim, gourd-shaped moon. Gossamer veils stream from the mottled surface, green-white jets of gas and dust. He's made this journey over a score and more of years, and never has such a light kindled in the dark. His heart pounds with an unreasoned joy as he leans back into the threadbare upholstery of his seat.

Had he been the first to see it? Pike glances around, experiencing a hot rush of shame for his foolish grin. He shouldn't worry. A-Deck is lightly populated, only a quarter of its time-chewed seats occupied. A stout farmer two rows in front of him coos to a babe squalling in his arms. A bespectacled financier across the aisle pays similar devotion to her datapad full of the latest reports from the Core. Some people just don't look up; they can't look out from their tiny lives to see the bigger picture.

Not like him.

Pike marvels again at the comet with another flush of joy. He laughs the way he used to when he and Mama played with the red worms that used to inch up the rusty stalks of wheat-sedge they grew on the farm.

But it's not just Mama he thinks of when he lays eyes on the strange comet. Not long ago, when his work brought him to and from Silas's Crossing more frequently, he fell into the missionary orbit of Brother Hong of the Gray Temple. The monk told him humanity's just like thin lines of ants marching into the vast fields of the cosmos where a combine waits to thresh them all. Pike believes that in the shifting stars and the weird glimmerings of warp space, the Nameless Ones are the waiting combine.

As a young man, Pike always chose practical matters over the spiritual. He took over the farm on Crockett when Mama died of the dry rot. He worked it on behalf of AgriGrow Corporation right up until they bought him out along with the whole southern continent. He got a thin payout and the uncertain promise of factory work at a fertilizer plant that never materialized. Instead, he joined a collective of farmers to fight for what remained of their rights against AGC's burgeoning control. Turns out, there wasn't much left to fight for, so he took his fight into the shadows. Company spies and mercs made his work dangerous, sometimes deadly. He'd lost count of how many corporates he'd killed on behalf of the collective. Corpos just like the woman across the aisle.

But age had eventually nudged him to his *true* calling and that chance meeting in a back-alley chapel on Silas's Crossing twelve years ago.

In addition to a new spiritual rapport, Brother Hong rekindled in Pike more *personal* feelings.

Between each passionate, breathless coupling, Pike begged Brother Hong to sing the final covenant of the Nameless Ones. Before they left the universe and vanished into warp space untold millennia before, it is said they left behind a promise of their own:

When the stars shine different from night to night,
When the moons spin 'round in spirals tight,
When unbidden gleams a comet light . . .
The Nameless Ones chant their ancient rite.

A children's rhyme, maybe, or Gray Temple doggerel, but doesn't Brother Hong teach that truth can rest in such simple rhyme?

Crockett's rocky moonlets have reached their fifty-year perigee relative to the planet. AGC's clumsy engineering of the wheat-sedge further destroys the ecology. Dry rot still kills hundreds of colonists on Crockett each year. And now, an uncharted comet—or perhaps something else—has appeared in the skies.

"Soon, Rance," Hong whispered, gently nibbling his earlobe on what proved to be their last night on Silas's Crossing, a year before. Mama'd said the same thing when he asked her if she was going to get better the day before she died. With her last breaths, she croaked out a similar verse:

When the seed won't sow from deadly blight,
And the sun burns out in fear of night,
Then shines anew that comet light . . .
The Nameless Ones reap their ancient right.

On their final visit, during the ceremony that marked Durance's education complete, Brother Hong gifted him a satchel, an antique bag of heavy brocade and worn leather. His eyes were misty.

"A seed for planting when the stars are different. Then, but not before, return to me, my brother," he'd said.

Pike carries the satchel wherever he goes, waiting for the right moment to prove his devotion. Even now, the bag sits cradled between Pike's booted feet, half stowed beneath the seat in front of him. It's a curious object inside the satchel, hardly anything like the bombs Pike planted in his previous career as an agitator, but Brother Hong says it will blast the old world apart all the same.

Is now that time? Is this strange celestial body outside the window a sign from the Nameless Ones? The furtive excitement washes over him again.

"What's that, Daddy?"

The toddler squirms out of the farmer's arms and points out their window. A chorus of audible gasps rises from the passenger deck. His fellow travelers have finally noticed.

"Well, I'll be!" her father exclaims. Pike wonders if they feel the same electric call in their hearts as he does.

One of the stewards, a lanky young woman with blonde hair shaved close to her skull, waves her arms for calm and tells everyone to remain seated. Only a routine course correction.

Bullshit. Pike doesn't buy it, and neither do many of the passengers. It's no mistake. They've been *called* here. The din of excited voices grows as people stand in their seats, demanding to know the reason for the delay, the explanation for that *thing* hanging in their path. A few stand gawping, faces pressed against the viewports.

They can't yet recognize it for what it must be—not just a comet but a herald from the Nameless Ones themselves. The commotion's a good excuse, however, to rise from his own seat and slip down the aisle before the flustered deckhand notices him.

Aft of the vending units, Pike locates a hatch down to the unused Passenger B-Deck. It's closed but unlocked, and no one is looking. The muffled and indistinct voice of the captain crackles through the tinny PA speakers as he slips down the stairs and dogs the hatch behind him. He hurries across the large, empty deck, a mirror to the one above, clutching his satchel tight. It's warm in his arms, his own facsimile of the farmer's child. The comet looms outside the windows, filling B-Deck with its wan, mysterious light. An electric thrill of certainty arcs once again through Durance Pike's long, lean frame.

Pike doesn't have a plan yet, but he needs some space to think things through. This is an opportune chance, perhaps his last, to prove to Brother Hong the depth of his faith. If it's in his power, he'll welcome the Nameless Ones back, just as he and Brother Hong had dreamed.

Maintenance ladderwells run like capillaries through the decks of the *Grass is Greener*. Plunging down one narrow shaft, Lira silently questions the shipwright who decided the primary sensor control room was best accessed from such inconvenient corridors. She floats in the null gravity outside the control room, waiting for Abe to arrive, glad for a moment's respite. The headache has not abated.

With a trembling hand, Lira withdraws a small med bulb from the pocket of her jumpsuit. The white liquid stimulant swirls inside, and though not specially formulated for her synthetic biology, it provides relief from the tremors and the headaches that result when she dwells too much on the events aboard the *Highline*.

She presses the stimbulb to her neck, and the auto injector hisses. At once, her headache subsides. She's reaching for another bulb when she hears rustling in the ladderwell above.

"Lira?" Abe calls down.

She just manages to shove the stimbulb back into her jumpsuit as the bioengineer comes drifting down. Abe is wrinkled and lithe, catlike, and completely at home in the cramped ladderwell, unlike Lira.

"Courtesy suggests you should have comm'd first," she protests as he slides next to her, the worn bladder of his tool bag slung over his shoulder.

Their shared bunk is only a little smaller than the ladderwell, but there, his touch is gentle and expected. Down here, their elbows and knees knock in a painful and clumsy intimacy. Abe winces when Lira inadvertently boxes his kidneys.

"Dammit, Lir, quit moving." A laugh chuckles up from his pain. Always laughing, Abe Mistri.

"Apologies, Abe," Lira says. "Perhaps I can calibrate the sensors myself."

There's little reason for them both to be in here when one pair of hands is as good as two. Abe gives her shoulder a gentle squeeze with his long fingers. She shivers, another human response.

"Let me help. Plus, the skipper asked me to check in on you."

"Unnecessary," she replies, a little brusquer than meant. She's practiced in hiding the shakes, but Abe knows her too well.

"It's getting worse, isn't it?"

"I don't know what you mean."

Lira turns to the access hatch, eager to exchange this conversation for the business of adjusting the main sensors.

Abe grins, a familiar response to her evasiveness. He reaches around her to help with the release clamps. They're sealed shut with age. The main sensors haven't been accessed from here in years. For the few minutes while they struggle with the hatch, Abe doesn't press his inquiry. With a grunt, Lira swings it free, and he returns to the subject.

"I've never heard you go off on Driscoll that way, Lir."

"He called my observations into question," she explains.

Abe laughs. "He calls *everyone's* observations into question, Lira. Even the skipper's when she's not around."

Abe leans close, smelling of engine grease and the musky perfume of ship's biotics. She flushes.

"You okay? You were about to inject again just now. This comet has you spooked."

She's never told Abe about the *Highline*, and now's not the time. No doubt Abe knows there's some sort of incident in her past. No experienced spacer, let alone a prized synthetic navigator, chooses service in the Mosquito Fleets over the bigger operations in the Core.

"The gravity is weird. I'm not sure that *is* a comet," she corrects Abe.

That quiets him. He narrows his eyes.

"What is it then?"

Lira floats into the control room, positioning herself before the central column that houses the main focusing dials. The column itself is mechanical, though it's wrapped in a skein of transparent conduits like blood vessels. Biomass, the circulatory lifeblood of the ship's biotic systems, pulses through the conduits, bathing the cabin in a soft cyan haze.

"An unknown navigational hazard," she replies with a small grin.

Abe shakes his head, laughing at her wry ambiguity.

Lira wonders sometimes if the bioengineer is attracted to her physical form or whether it's her personification of the biotic systems that he loves. It certainly can't be her wit, she's surmised.

As Abe opens his tool bag and extracts a gel wand, Lira unlatches the control panel.

"I'm concerned about the skipper, Abe," she says, which is mostly the truth at least. "She's sicker than she admits."

Abe shrugs sadly. He's noticed it too.

"Treatment's expensive, yeah. But she's got years ahead of her, Lir."

"But what happens when she dies? Or retires?"

"No reason we can't stay aboard *Grass is Greener*. You'd make a fine skipper too," he adds.

It's her turn to laugh.

"Driscoll might disagree."

It's not really command she worries about. Synthetics aren't unknown as ships' masters, though they usually serve in specialized roles aboard more advanced vessels than *Grass is Greener*. No, she worries more about the secret Juarez keeps and about who might learn it when she dies.

Can't worry about it now. Lira turns her attention to the sensors. On the control port, tiny veins of biomass flow around the controls, feeding nutrients to the biotic sensor fronds and sending sensor impulses back to the ship.

Abe peels back a safety valve with his wand, allowing Lira to comb the fine hairs on the detection stalks.

A small holo displays the results of their labors. There's still a lot of grain in the signal, but the enhanced outlines of the main comet show very little additional debris to be concerned about. The unusually strong gravity, Lira thinks, is another matter entirely.

A tremulous whine surges through the control column—the noise a silver spike in Lira's already tender skull. She gasps. The feedback reminds her of the static that blasted through Driscoll's headset earlier.

"That's not background radiation," she frowns.

"What's not background radiation?" Abe says, puzzled and concerned.

"You didn't hear that?" Lira's chest turns icy and hollow.

Abe shakes his head.

"When's the last time you had your aural nodes checked?" he asks. "I've got my forceps. We could take a look now." The bioengineer reaches for his bag.

Lira turns away angrily. Maybe that's the whole reason Abe's with her. Advanced synthetic biology in a human package. A ship he can talk to. Fuck. She frowns at the uncharitable thought.

"I'm sorry, Lir. I could adjust . . . something else instead?" He laughs, not realizing how ill-timed his joke is.

"I'm not a ship, Abe," she snaps.

Abe's eyes widen at her rebuke. Anger flares in his eyes briefly before softening to remorse. "I'm sorry, Lira. You know I don't see you that way."

"I know," she replies without much conviction. If her head wasn't caught in an invisible vice, she might have more to say to him. They'd have to talk about it soon though. After they got underway again. After another stimbulb.

"I am. Truly," he says.

Abe opens his arms wide but low. A gesture of contrition.

"Yeah."

She hugs him loosely. He allows it.

"It's okay," she says, pulling him tighter. He's not lying about his feelings, at least not to her. For a moment, she forgets the headache roaring in her ears. But as Lira holds Abe Mistri close, she feels the stimbulb pressing against her thigh.

Alone at the sink in the aft passenger lavatory of the empty B-Deck, Pike gazes on Brother Hong's strange gift with something like disappointment. The object is a tapered ovoid of black glass as long as his forearm. Scalloped plates or scales rib the surface with subtle ridges. Glittering just beneath the ribs, flecks of jade sparkle like miniature constellations. Truthfully, for all the weight Brother Hong had invested in the gift, it looks like nothing more than a knick-knack, a mass-produced pretty for the tourists on an Oleander beach. This, *this*, is supposed to blast apart the universe?

He lifts it from the satchel. It's heavy and cool in his hands, just as he expects a lump of glass to be. What had Brother Hong called it? A shell, a seed, a *spore*.

Pike catches his reflection in the mirror and feels ridiculous. His face burns with shame. He's just an old man mooning over an ex-lover's trinket. Why should his promises to that bald monk even matter now?

Because you have to honor the love you once shared, Rance. Because the stars are different tonight.

The words come to Pike in his mama's voice, and it bothers him. He's never allowed that sort of treacly sentimentality to infect him. He did have faith in the Nameless Ones though. Or at least an admiration for their cold indifference to the world they'd left behind.

Gazing on the oddity up close makes Pike sweat, and his eyelids droop as if weighed down by stones. An impression of unimaginable age washes over him, making his eighty-five years seem young in comparison. Something flutters deep within the glassy object, numbing his fingers. He shoves the "spore" back into the satchel and clasps it shut. The feeling of weariness ebbs, but the disquieting pressure on his fingertips lingers. *That's never happened before.*

Brother Hong spoke of the legacy of the Nameless Ones, but Pike always reckoned he was just talking stories, not artifacts. Could this spore be picking up some sort of signal from that comet or whatever out there? A tingle passes from his fingertips and down his spine. It's the thrill he gets just before he moves on a target. Not exactly a confirmation of the theory, but Pike's learned to trust his gut.

He closes his eyes, trying to imagine the civilization of the Nameless Ones that Brother Hong described between sultry afternoon couplings: entire planets covered in gargantuan towers, vast astronomical temple complexes that stretched from horizon to horizon, science and technology beyond the childish concerns of grasping corporation and indigent farmer. Starships the size of moons—or comets.

Is that what spins in the dark outside this decrepit ferry?

A sudden ache to gaze upon the frosty prominences of the mysterious comet overwhelms him. He mumbles the almost forgotten prayers Brother Hong taught him—a rough approximation of the ancient tongue, he'd said. *Will the prayers be enough? Will they accept the offerings?* Brother Hong must have thought so, or he would not have given him care of the Star Spore.

How to get to the comet, he wonders. Short of wresting control of *Grass is Greener* from the crew, that is. He's too old for that shit. But the captain announced plans to fire the engines again soon to put them on a wider course around it. He can't permit that, no. Not until he decides what to do.

The years with the collective taught him a few things about industrial sabotage. A ferry isn't all that different from a grain barge after all. Unplug the right conduits, override the pressure valves on the biomass pumps—throw a wrench into the works. No one would suspect sabotage, not until he'd made his move anyway.

Pike may not be able to stop the ferry from leaving, but maybe he can slow them down. He smiles at the old man grinning in the mirror. The Nameless Ones waited millennia to return. Time is on his side.

The crew-only passageways of the ferry are even more careworn than the passenger decks. Illumination panels flicker dimly overhead. Status lights wink from countless recesses like rainbow eyes. Fanning across the machined bulkheads, veins of nurturing biomass pulse with their sluggish blue light. Pike might wander through *Grass is Greener* at his leisure for quite some time before a crew member challenges him. Even so, he keeps to the shadows that pool in the stanchions that line the passageways. Better not to be spotted at all.

Following standard nautical markings along the deck, Pike passes an airlock, then an equipment locker, and through a junction to the hatch for the engineering compartment. Once again, while secured, the hatch is not locked.

Pike's learned to be suspicious when things are easy. He tenses, expecting an ambush. None comes. Could the Nameless Ones be clearing his way?

The engineering compartment is not much larger than Brother Hong's cell back on Silas's Crossing. Control boards ring a sunken pit where the twin housings of the sublight engines squat like giant sarcophaguses. The roar of machinery fills his ears, and control boards glitter like jewels in the half-light. Biomass conduits sprout like mighty trees here, roots and branches snaking away into the overhead to biotic junctions throughout the ship. Their music throbbing deep in his bones. In the satchel he clutches to his chest, the spore echoes the vibrations, a second heartbeat to his own...

Pike snaps from his trance, realizing too late he's forgotten to check if the compartment is occupied. But no. He's alone here. Fate or coincidence?

His skin crawls as he climbs to the nearest control board. Droplets of sweat bead along his thin hairline. He doesn't like coincidence. Excitement or panic arcs through him like lightning. His heart hammers at his ribcage, too fast for his age. He feels dizzy.

Pike traces a nest of ordinary electrical wires running from the control board to a nearby biomass exchanger. The biotic ring contains a half-dozen semi-organic and mechanical valves. It squats in the center of a spiderweb of flow-regulation circuitry.

Pike cuts the power to the exchanger, allowing a volatile mix of energy and biomass to build up in the valves. In response, several amber lights wink on.

There's a failsafe in place to keep the engines and biotic systems from overloading though. He eyes the hefty mechanical lock that protects the failsafe switch and then glances around for a wrench or something equally heavy to smash the lock. Despite the worn condition of the ferry though, the tools are kept out of sight.

He's not going to shut down the engines that way. No doubt one of the engineering mates has a key, but he can't wait in the engine compartment until they find him. More yellow warnings flash on the control board as pressure begins to build.

He studies the biotic ring again. In the center is a diagnostic port, a rubbery spigot for sampling the health of the biomass. Its opening is a knotted sphincter of synth muscle, but it would easily yield for maintenance.

Plant a seed, Brother Hong had said.

Tenderly, Pike removes the spore from his satchel. He could shove it into the port. At the worst, it might block the biomass flow and lead to a temporary paralysis of the biotic systems in engineering. At most? Well, if the spore were truly an artifact of the Nameless Ones, then maybe it would do more.

As he works it into the port, warm biomass leaks over his hands. The scent is vegetal with a floral spice. The spore lodges in the throat of the spigot, able to go no farther. It reminds him of the time one of his sows gave birth and one of her piglets became lodged in the birth canal. He'd saved the mother but not the baby. Pike flushes with embarrassment. *A stupid idea for a stupid old fool.*

As he withdraws his hands, the spore cracks, and chunks of the iridescent stone spill out on the deck. The main portion remains caught though, oozing a dark-green liquid, thick as molasses. It mingles with the biomass, foaming and turning it black.

Saint's asshole, what is that?

One by one, all the warning lights on the regulator console flick to red. Pike holds his breath. The roar of the engines modulates, getting deeper. Greasy black foam drips from the spigot, and all around the biotic exchanger, the biomass turns inky.

"Hey! Who the fuck are you?"

Pike spins from the engineering console, cursing his distraction. One of the engineers is climbing the stairs to the console's platform—a kid practically, clad in a sorry gray rag of a jumpsuit. He's bald save for a blond topknot striped with crimson dye. One of his eyes is cybernetic, a radiant green jewel that's most likely a computer interface. He's brandishing a gasket punch like a club, and his smooth-shaven face is contorted in anger.

Pike sighs. He knows all too well what comes next.

Lira pulls away from the awkward embrace with Abe. His dark eyes cloud with worry. She looks past him to the control column. Blips of data march around the screen like ants as the sensors update the course corrections for the comet and its debris field. The larger fragments remain safely clustered around the main mass, but the data reveal something more troubling.

"Hmm."

"What *hmm*?" Abe says, pulling fully away. He's stooped slightly like he's expecting a physical blow. *He thinks I'm still talking about us.* There's no time for that right now.

She tips her chin at the screen behind him. Abe's eyes widen, and he turns to follow her gaze.

"What am I looking at?"

"We've changed course again, Abe," she says, tracing the projections with a finger. "Observe our vectors here and here. We're falling into the comet's orbit. Just like those debris fragments."

"Impossible. We steered around it, and the gravity isn't strong enough to pull us in."

"And yet," she says. Lira frowns. She'd just plotted their new course. Why were they reverting to the old one? "Perhaps I miscalculated again."

"Impossible," Abe repeats, but this time he doesn't seem as sure.

Confusion paralyzes her, and she gazes at the sensor data without really seeing it.

"Damn, Lir, you're right," Abe says, tapping on the screen as if that would change anything.

"There's some residual warp space folding," she concedes.

"Yeah," he says, "but not from us. Our wake's dissipated."

"Right," Lira scoffs, "These readings suggest it shunted in and out of warp space. Comets don't do that."

The comm buzzes.

"Hey, Abe," Magnus Lin sounds annoyed.

"I'm getting some weird fluctuations on the mains. Did you fire the engines again?"

"No, Mags," Abe replies. "I've been working on the sensors with Lira. Wait, aren't *you* in engineering?"

"Not yet. Was helping Callum with some passengers. A couple were headed toward an airlock, and another group was trying to stop them."

"What?"

"I guess they panicked and thought it was a lifepod."

"What's there to panic about?" Abe muses, studying the sensor data.

"Nothing. That's what we told them. They seemed confused, but I think we got it sorted. So hey, I'm almost to engineering now, Abe. Help me take a look at these fluctuations?"

Lira nods. *Yes, please.*

"Sure, Mags. Just, er, finishing up here. Maintain dead slow until I get back there. We might still be riding some spacetime eddies."

"Right-o. See you in a few." Lin crackles out.

"I should go back to the bridge and inform Juarez," Lira says, turning for the long climb back toward the bridge. Abe opens his mouth to say something, but whatever it is, he holds his tongue. The personal mysteries will have to wait until the present anomalies are bypassed.

Abe's mouth quirks in a sad smile, and he leads the way out of the control room, gliding up the handholds of the ladderwell ahead of her.

Lira follows slowly, allowing the distance between her and Abe to grow. He senses her reticence, picking up speed to give her the space she's silently asking for.

A square of bluish light above marks the end of the maintenance shaft and the main corridor. Abe slips out onto the main deck a good ten meters ahead of her.

"See you soon?" he calls down without looking back.

"I'll be right there. Checking on something."

Abe nods and vanishes from sight.

Lira pulls out the stimbulb only for it to fly from her shaking hands. There's no time to curse before the bulkheads leap at her, slamming into her from the right and then the left. She tumbles back down the zero-g ladderwell. The impacts wrap a flickering gauze across her vision. Somewhere above, Abe shouts, but his cries are soon lost in a groan of tearing metal that follows her into sudden and complete darkness.

The warning lights reflect in the engineer's streaky topknot, and for one moment, it reminds Pike of the way the neon light used to shine in Brother Hong's tonsure in the Bhindar marketplace. Pike feels a rare pang. He kicks—his old legs still plenty strong for all his moaning. The engineer slams against the overloading console with a grunt. Pike draws a knife from his boot.

The engineer recovers fast, grabbing a nearby gasket punch. He lunges, and while honed instincts roll Pike away from the thrust, he's not quick enough. The tool punctures a hole in his duster and slides into his left side, just below the ribs.

A cold fire roars through Pike's side. Pain chokes off his breath. The engineer rocks back, triumph and terror mingling in his eyes. It's a fatal pause, and one Pike's quick to exploit. He throws his knife, and the blade buries itself in the engineer's neck. He drops like a stone after that, the heavy tool clattering to the deck.

Pike slips down too. Lands with a thud against the ruined console. When he finds the strength to right himself, his duster is caked with a paste of gore—his own and the ship's. Blood and biomass. Lightheaded, Pike hurls himself down the access corridor, limping back toward the shuttered B-Deck. The pain burns him. It freezes his blood.

A sharp violence rocks the ferry, a sudden quake of acceleration. Pike crumples into a bulkhead. Searing pain tears at his consciousness. The metal frame of *Grass is Greener* shrieks in torment as the ship twists under the force of several gees.

He pants on the deck, wondering when the chaos and pain will cease and whether the Nameless Ones will be waiting on the other side of it.

Unconsciousness lasts only moments. Lira's synthetic brain, with neurons designed for sudden fluctuations in gravity and spacetime, brings her back to a full if fuzzy alertness. She floats in a cloud of microdebris, the accumulation of ages of dirt shed by the ladderwell.

Had Grass is Greener *hit something? A fragment of the comet?*

Pink globules of synthetic blood form constellations around Lira's head, yet she feels no new pain, just the tightening fist of her headache.

Where's the stim, she thinks. Followed quickly by, *Where's Abe?*

She gets the answer to the former right away. The stimbulb floats into view, a twinkling star pulsing in the amber calamities of emergency lights.

Lira snatches the bulb, lets the auto injector do its work. Her mind blazes like a floodlight, clearing the shadows of the headache and sharpening her predicament: head down in the gravity-neutral ladderwell with her leg caught on a torn rung. The twisted metal has opened a gash in her right calf, exposing purple muscle and gunmetal bone. Her body has rerouted the pain for now, but it will come soon, most likely along with the self-judgment for choosing the stimbulb first over Abe.

Warning lights throb beyond her immediate position, relentless blooms of red and yellow. A terrible silence from above, interrupted only by her shallow breaths.

Lira twists, trying to see up to the passage where Mistri had been only moments before. She flicks away the ampoule, disgusted. The shame momentarily anchors her in the maintenance tube, but she shrugs away the momentary indecision and pulls herself up the rungs.

"Abe!" Moving quickly makes her dizzy, or maybe it's the stim. She wobbles into the passageway, blinking into the strobing lights. Distant klaxons wail.

To her immense relief, Abe's waiting for her with a pained grin.

"Hey, Lir."

The bioengineer's wedged himself between bulkhead stanchions, his long limbs braced against the motion of the stricken ferry, which is spinning. And Lira realizes that is responsible for her sudden dizzy spell.

"Saints of grace," she says, crawling toward him. Her wounded leg stiffens with pain as the immediate rush of the stim wanes.

She clasps Abe close, drifting in the motion of the ship. *We're rolling.*

"You okay, Lira?"

Abe's dark eyes linger where her jumpsuit is torn and slick.

"Synthetic nerves. The pain is minimal," she lies.

Abe winces as she lightly touches the wound on his forehead. The gash shines with fresh blood.

"Superficial," she diagnoses. The bioengineer had suffered worse injuries playing voidball.

"Did we just accelerate?" Abe wonders aloud.

"Improbable. The *Grass is Greener* isn't rated for gees that extreme."

"And yet," Abe echoes her from before.

A more likely explanation is that they hit a cometary fragment the sensors didn't see. If so, it's another error on her part. Headaches and stims aside, it defies her comprehension that she's capable of making these sorts of mistakes.

Perhaps it shouldn't, she thinks darkly, remembering Adamson A621. It's no time for self-recrimination though. Ship's counting on her.

Lira punches up the bridge on the comm unit mounted on the wall.

"Captain, this is the chief mate. What's our status, over?"

Static's her only reply. That and a fresh burst of the semi-melodic chirps Driscoll had first heard. The interference was disturbing the internal comms now too.

"Is the bridge still . . . there?" Abe's not usually one to indulge in extreme speculation. Lira gives him a questioning look.

"It was a hell of an acceleration," Abe mutters, scratching the top of his head and gingerly avoiding his scrape.

His uncharacteristic anxiety is infectious. Lira feels her chest tighten along with her skull.

"Bridge, this is Chief Mate Lira and Engineer Mistri reporting in. What's our status, over?"

After almost a minute more of static, Driscoll's voice, thick with fear, stammers over the channel.

"Saints of s-shit. Y'all better get up here," he says.

Beyond the viewports of the bridge, the rogue comet looms dead ahead, the glimmering streams of its gas haunting the bridge like circling ghosts. *Grass is Greener* is indeed rolling on its centerline, spiraling ever closer to the comet's soot-frosted surface.

Alerts for every system are sounding in the narrow bridge. Loss of main power. Engines down and unresponsive. Degradation of biotic function up to 35 percent and rising. Artificial gravity failing in random sections. It's all bad news.

But the worst of it is that Captain Juarez is dead.

Whatever accident had caused the sudden, out-of-control lurch hurled the skipper into the diamond-hard viewport at several gees. She floats there still, neck broken. Drops of blood trail from her half-open mouth, and her milky gray eyes are wide with surprise.

"Oh shit-fucking saints," Abe gasps.

The captain's death slams Lira like a physical blow.

It was supposed to be cancer.

Lira moves to go to her, but another thought stops her cold.

We hadn't finished negotiating the end of my service.

If there was anything more to come out about Lira's role in the *Highline* disaster, it would be from Juarez's final testament. Juarez's death either means Lira's secret is hers alone or it's about to go public. But perhaps none of them will survive today, meaning it will hardly matter.

Lira, vexed by this trend toward human fatalism, clears her thoughts to focus on the surviving quartermaster.

"I t-tried to grab her," Driscoll says, pale as the comet light.

"At those gees, you wouldn't have been able to stop her," Lira replies, corkscrewing across the bridge deck to grab hold of the skipper. Her body is still warm but cooling fast. Damnit.

Farewell, Erinn.

"Status report, Pete," she commands, gently closing Juarez' eyes and mouth and swallowing the sharp taste of grief at the back of her throat.

"W-what?"

"*Status report*, Driscoll," She snaps, trying to cut through the shock that surrounds the quartermaster like a fog. Lira secures the skipper's body against a lower bulkhead.

Juarez deserves the airlock for what she's done to you.

The savage impulse flashes through Lira's mind. Perhaps Juarez took advantage of Lira's situation, but the skipper had saved her from a worse imprisonment or termination after the *Highline*. Juarez always looked after her crew. Now, it's Lira's turn.

Abe, good engineer that he is, is already at his station, firing thrusters and slowing the ferry's drunken roll. He scans the chaos of error lights and scrolling holos to make some sense of their predicament.

"Main engines still down, but we have auxiliary power and life support. Hmm," he frowns. "Looks like there was a blockage in the main biotic arteries."

"The ship had a heart attack?" Driscoll exclaims, recovering himself enough to study his own console.

"Something like that. But it doesn't explain the acceleration toward the comet."

"Again, if it *is* a comet," Lira says.

"Whatever the hell it is, we're going to hit it unless we change course," Driscoll warns.

"Did we hit a fragment?"

"Nah. *You* didn't see anything, remember, Lira?" Driscoll's shock has gone, replaced by anger.

"Captain," she corrects him. "I'm assuming command per ship's charter."

Abe suppresses a smile, but Driscoll's eyebrows shoot up.

"Like fucking hell!"

"It's true, Pete," Abe says quietly. "Chief mate is acting skipper in the case of death or incapacitation."

"She made the fucking mistake that got us in this mess," Driscoll protests. "Now, you want her to take command?"

Lira inclines her head, acknowledging Driscoll's concerns to a point.

"And yet concerning navigational matters, there's no more qualified crew aboard."

"Bullshit—" Driscoll starts.

"Pete—" Abe interjects.

Saints of shit, how did Juarez handle this?

"Both of you, please. I need you. Driscoll, any luck raising Crockett control?"

"I've been trying, *Skipper*," he says, sullen. "None. That damn interference. It's either the comet or a fault in the ship. I can't tell." Driscoll dons a headset and starts flipping through the channels again.

"Thanks, Pete. Keep trying."

"Aye, *sir*."

Lira turns to Abe. "So how we doing?"

"Better than a minute ago," Abe reports. "Artificial gravity is coming back on most decks and life support is holding on all decks. Biotic systems down to only 15 percent degradation. *Grass is Greener* is healing itself."

"What about our passengers," she asks, dreading the response. Neither ship nor crew can afford legal action.

Driscoll punches up A-Deck cams.

The ferry carries only seventy-five out of a possible three-hundred passengers on this run, a fortunate circumstance. Lira shudders to think what might have happened if both decks were full.

As it is, there's enough to be concerned about. Passengers crouch in their seats, sobbing. Some lay in the aisles, wincing when they try to move. A corporate wipes her bloody forehead with her scarf. A farmer holds his little girl close. A rangy colonist in a black farmer's duster staggers toward a lavatory, his bag clutched to his chest. Scanning past him to other channels, Lira spots two of the deckhands, trying to corral a group of passengers standing gawp-mouthed at the observation ports back in their seats and mostly failing. Fortunately, it doesn't look like anyone else was killed.

"We're not the only ones shook up," Driscoll mutters, glancing at Juarez's body.

The statement heralds the full return of Lira's headache. Every click and shriek on the malfunctioning comms magnifies in her skull.

I really should have Abe take a look at me, Lira realizes.

"What does Mags report?" she asks the bioengineer instead.

"Haven't heard from him yet," Abe replies.

He doesn't say what they're all thinking: *Why not?*

Lira slouches in Juarez's seat, pressing the comm switch.

"Lin, this is the bridge. C'mon, Mags, answer."

Abe stands, grabbing his engineer's satchel from its hook at his station.

"I'm going down there," he says. "The trouble with the engines has to have originated there."

"I'll go too. Pete, you stay here."

"And do what, Captain? Watch us hit the goddamn comet? I can't steer this fucking boat without engines."

"Stay on those thrusters and do your best. Keep trying to raise Crockett. Let us know if anything changes."

"We gotta get to the lifepods, Captain," Driscoll says, a pleading note in his suggestion.

He surprises Lira. Pete Driscoll's a quarrelsome son-of-a-bitch, but he loves the *Grass is Greener* despite all his discontent. He's got to be terrified to suggest abandoning the ship so quickly.

"That's a premature course of action, Driscoll," she says, testing him. "*Grass is Greener* is hardly lost."

Driscoll glares at her as if deciding once again to challenge her leadership. He relents, shrugging.

"The comet, Skipper. Or whatever the hell it is. We're getting caught in the tug of those gravitational waves. If we wait to launch the pods when we're further in . . ." he tapers off, letting her imagine the results.

It's a fair point, Lira admits to herself.

"Very well. Activate the pre-launch cycles on the pods. We'll have them ready just in case."

"Thanks, Lira," Driscoll says.

She softens her tone. When Driscoll isn't mouthing off, he's a capable officer. "It's a good suggestion, Pete. Just no evac orders until I give them, okay?"

Driscoll nods, mollified.

Abe clears his throat, and Lira catches him looking at his hands.

"What's your vote, Abe?"

Driscoll glances up sharply, cutting a look to the engineer.

Lira wonders where the bioengineer's mind is, caught between devotion to his ship, his concern for the passengers, and his loyalty to his lover.

"Pete's right, Lira. It's good to be prepared." The quartermaster smiles and ducks his head in vindication.

"But evacuation?" Abe continues. That's up to you . . . *sir*. You're the skipper now."

Durance Pike leans against the lavatory door, trying to stay upright. Every breath is a mouthful of fire, yet his side seems encased in ice. His nostrils are full of a musty, faintly ammoniac odor. He can't tell if it comes from him or the ship.

He's bleeding like a stuck pig and *goddamn* it hurts. He tucks his hand under his duster, and his fingers come away in a paste of gore and curdled biomass. The ammonia smell intensifies.

So it's him then.

The edges of his vision gray out, and Pike remembers the day AGC came to the farm—the same day, in fact, that Mama died. The rep's air car touched down in the dry field just as Mama started hollering from the house.

"Rance! Rance! I need you, Son!"

The last time she'd ever called out to him, it turned out. He can almost hear her calling now. Pike wipes blood from his fingers, but the black biomass remains. Tiny flecks of green shine in his skin when he turns his hands in the light.

Shit. All over me.

Lucky there's a sink close by. He'll clean up and figure out what to do next. Got to be some way to get over to the comet. Maybe find a lifepod or at least an EVA suit and wait for the ship to drift closer. Pike pushes through the door.

This time, he's not alone in the lavatory. A young man wearing a ship's jumpsuit steadies himself against the metal sink. Blood drips from the curls of his fine, mouse-brown hair. In the mirror, his blue eyes are dull. The man's lips move with silent words. Prayer? Agitation wells up in Pike, and he feels for the knife he no longer has.

The deckhand goes back to staring at himself in the mirror, too self-absorbed to pay any heed to Pike.

Pike sequesters himself in the same stall he'd hidden in before. Fresh pain lances out from his side, and Pike lurches against the divider. He'd been shot by corporate agents countless times, staggered around with the shards of their needlers in his belly. He shattered his legs jumping from a Bhindar factory roof once. Nothing ever hurt this bad though.

Pike removes his duster and fingers the edges of the wound with careful prodding. The blood is black and sticky, mingling with biomass. Tiny green puffs stick to his fingers.

What the hell? He takes a deep, shuddering breath that opens an icy hole into nothing.

"Attention, passengers."

A voice on the PA, muddied in a wave of static. A woman, but it doesn't sound like the captain.

"We've sustained an engine malfunction, but there is no cause for alarm. The crew is assessing the damage, and we've sent word to Crockett. We anticipate a delay in arrival but expect to be underway shortly. Please follow crew commands and return to your seats."

"Chief mate's lying," mutters the young deckhand at the sink.

Chief mate? Where's the captain?

"Deckhands, please report to the bridge for further instruction."

"No, sir. I can hear the music better here," the deckhand whispers.

What music? Pike thinks. The crackling over the comm is almost a melody, but—

The ship spins again. This time though, the rolling is all in Pike's head. He crashes to the floor, the dim spark of his awareness caught in the tide of the swirling lavatory lights.

The roaring reminds Pike of the seasonal winds that swept across their farm. Destructive, yes, but also bringers of the rain the crops so desperately needed after a long, dry summer. A shadow flickers at the edge of his vision.

Mama? he wonders.

The stall door bounces open, and the young man's lean brown face hovers inches away. A cold sweat sheens his brow.

"You're not supposed to be in here, mister." His accent is clipped, mid-continent Silas's Crossing. Probably a factory kid. The dull light in his eyes has cleared, but he still looks dazed.

"Here I am," Pike grunts or at least believes he does. He's not sure he actually speaks the words.

"Saints, sir. You're hurt. Bad."

He reaches out with sturdy arms, but Pike slaps them away.

"Leave me be," Pike growls.

"You need medical attention, sir," the deckhand insists, not unkindly.

True enough. Pike'll bleed out if he doesn't find a way to close his wound. Somehow, deep within the disused lavatory, he can feel the pressure of the comet's dark light. He doesn't want to die now. Not here.

The PA speaker crackles, emitting the same high-pitched fluting before going silent again.

"Can you hear that?" the young man asks, eyes wide.

Pike nods. The kid looks relieved.

Pike wheezes with indecision. The kid's dazzle-eyed. Maybe he can help him.

"Got a medkit?" Pike grunts.

The deckhand shakes his head.

"Not on me, Mr. . . . ah?"

"Pike." Why the hell does he give the kid his name?

"I'm Roberto, Mr. Pike," the deckhand says. He cocks his head again to listen to the static. For a moment, Pike wonders if he forgets he's there.

"Don't like your captain much, do you?" Pike says in an attempt to bring him back.

"Oh, you mean Lira? She's not the captain. She's the chief mate. A synthetic. Our navigator."

A synthetic? Pike's blood goes cold. Independent vessels like this ferry usually couldn't afford a synth. They rated well, but upkeep was expensive. Beyond that, if this chief mate is a military model, Pike'll have to be extra careful. Some corporations hid them among the employees to keep trouble down. Stronger, faster than humans, you didn't tussle with them unless you were well prepared. Pike's hardly in great shape.

"I can get you back to your seat. The music's louder out by the viewports," Roberto offers. He glances over his shoulder again.

"No."

The moment he's caught in the open, his mission is over. It's bad enough he blundered into this addled kid's path, but there's still time to fix that. He grabs the front of the deckhand's coveralls and yanks him close.

"Is there a med bay?"

Roberto tries to free himself, but Pike's grip is iron.

Another stab of ice through his lungs dims Pike's world by a few lumens. He tugs the deckhand even closer.

"Answer me!"

Roberto nods. "There's a crew infirmary, sir. I can take you there, but we should go out and listen to the music first."

Pike shakes his head again. No, no. Time for that soon enough. "You . . . have . . . the . . . key?"

Roberto tries once more to wiggle free. "I do, sir. But if I take you there without—"

Pike surges to his feet, decades of well-honed survival instincts driving his limbs where his will cannot. He grips Roberto by the neck, feeling the kid's soft flesh part beneath his fingernails.

"I'll take it then," Pike gasps. Hurtling from the stall, he slams the man against the cheap mirror hung above the sink. The glass shatters into spiderweb mandalas.

The deckhand's amber eyes bulge as he fights to draw breath. Pike ignores his kicking feet.

Pike doesn't want to kill him. The presence of the Nameless Ones is clearly affecting his mind. Perhaps he could even be an ally. But Pike doesn't like partners. Creeping through the passageways of the ferry is much easier by yourself.

Pike drops the kid, cracking the back of his skull once more on the sink. The deckhand's amber eyes flick shut for the last time.

May the Nameless Ones grant you purpose.

Pike pats Roberto's jumpsuit and finds his keybadge in the breast pocket. There's also a small, steel flask in his right pants pocket. It's not standard issue, but neither is the sedge moonshine inside it. He gulps it all down, a restorative nip. Death retreats a few centimeters. It's enough for now.

Exhaustion and pain flood through Pike, but the tingle of excitement, of destiny, remains. The Nameless Ones brought Roberto to him, didn't they? He grimaces through fresh waves of agony. As long as he can stay on his feet until he gets to the infirmary, he'll find something that'll keep him going. Fleshwrap. Biogel. Painkillers. Stims.

Maybe all the above.

Something to push the void away until he's ready for it.

Pike leaves the lavatory, leaning on the wall for support. B-Deck is still empty, silent save for the distant hum and pulse of the biotic life-support systems. Through the forward observation ports, the comet shines its ghastly light. True to Roberto's word, the crackling and warbling in the PA does get louder, but Pike resists the temptation to stop and listen. If it is the voices of the Nameless Ones themselves, calling the believers to their embrace, then Pike will join them soon enough. Everyone aboard will.

He slinks once again into the maze of passageways, dangling Roberto's keybadge on his wrist, vowing to greet the Nameless Ones on his feet. Brother Hong would be proud.

No cause for alarm.

Not entirely accurate, Lira reflects, setting the PA handset back in its cradle.

She sinks into the command couch at the rear of the bridge—*her* command couch now, *her* bridge. The old cushions are too soft, making it impossible to sit up straight. How did Juarez see everything from back here? There are still signs of her on the console: timetables in the skipper's cribbed and spidery hand, a faded picture of a sunny Oleander beach, a crumpled foil packet that once contained chemo pills. Somehow Juarez's duty pad is still resting on the console where she left it, displaying a crossword puzzle that will never be finished.

43 Down. Six letter word for "in trouble."

Lira's fingers tremble for a stimbulb. This time, she faces disaster without Juarez. There's no one to lie for her in the inevitable inquest should *Grass is Greener* be lost today. She doesn't really know any of the deckhands, and Magnus Lin is a colleague, not a close friend. Pete Driscoll, of course, couldn't be relied on for a kind word most days. What about Abe though? Would the bioengineer lie about her navigational errors?

She's not sure she wants that either. Abe's been a good friend—and convenient bunkmate—but lately Lira's had some reservations about the basis of their relationship. It might be unwise to build on that foundation with a mortar of secrets. It hadn't worked so well for her and Erinn.

An explosion of noise heralds the deckhands through the main hatch and onto the bridge. Callum is rangy and lanky, like most spacers, with a dusting of blonde hair that makes her narrow head more cadaverous than it might otherwise present. The woman has a steady hand though—and an easy charm that belies her sickly appearance. Nasr's stout where Callum's tall, and she wears her hair long, though done up in a ponytail. The women are arguing as they enter.

"Callum, you can't rough passengers up like that," Nasr protests.

"They were ignoring crew instructions," Callum says calmly. "Standing in the viewport gawping at the comet while the ship was rolling. Someone could've gotten hurt."

"But you started shoving."

"Only because that one bastard took a swing."

"Callum, I want to hear more about these unruly passengers," Lira orders.

The pair come to attention, looking in confusion at Lira and then to Driscoll.

"Sir?" Callum says. It dawns on the junior deckhand where Lira's sitting.

"The skipper's dead, killed in the accident. I'm in command of the *Grass is Greener* now." There's little use sugarcoating it.

Nasr starts, finally noticing Juarez's body still strapped to the bulkhead. "Saints of shit," Nasr cries. She leans against the bulkhead, wracked with sobs. Skipper always had a thing for Fidda Nasr, and the feelings were mutual. And as secret as her relationship with Abe. Lira regrets her brusqueness. She allows

Nasr a moment to compose herself. Callum puts a tentative and awkward arm around her shipmate.

"Where's Roberto DeSouza?" Lira asks them. Doe-Eyed DeSouza, Juarez called him, though she kept their relationship strictly professional. In truth, Lira wonders why the skipper had hired him on in the first place. Roberto DeSouza has a small chip on his shoulder that with enough time aboard *Grass is Greener* seems likely to grow as large as Driscoll's.

Nasr and Callum exchange worried glances.

"We haven't seen him, sir," Callum says.

"Not since the accident," Nasr sniffs, unable to keep her eyes from the captain's body.

Driscoll looks up from his console in alarm, but he keeps his mouth shut.

Saints of shit. Juarez dead. Lin *and* DeSouza missing. Synthetics, as a rule, take a dim view of human concepts like fate or destiny, but Lira begins to consider that perhaps the universe may be more antagonistic than she has allowed.

"When's the last time you saw DeSouza?"

"Right before the ship rolled," Callum says. "He was securing the hatches to B-Deck. He found one standing open."

"He didn't find any passengers on B-Deck, did he?" Lira asks, worried the situation might be more complex than she'd thought.

"I don't know, Lir—er, Captain. I didn't see him after the impact."

It wouldn't do to have passengers wandering loose on B-Deck. There are hatches to the crew-only sections of the ship down there and not enough crew to watch them all.

"What about the skipper?" Callum asks, interrupting her thoughts.

"Take her to the forward cargo hold."

Nasr starts sobbing again. Lira furrows her brow. Perhaps Nasr would be a poor choice for that particular duty.

"No, I mean how did she die?" Callum asks.

"The accident flung her into the viewports," Driscoll said. "I couldn't grab her in time." Is that guilt in his voice?

Nasr glares at Driscoll through tear-filled eyes. The quartermaster turns away.

"I'm acting skipper," Lira informs them, "at least until we make it back to Crockett."

"Will we? Make it back, I mean?" Nasr's eyes are shining not just with grief but also fear.

"We will."

She means it. She's going to get the crew out of this mess. Maybe then they'll back her the way they backed Juarez.

Driscoll can't hold back his trademark derisive snort.

"More to say, Driscoll?"

"No sir, Skipper, sir."

Driscoll, realizing he doesn't have another fight in him, lets it drop.

"Callum, you and Driscoll take the captain out. Nasr, I need you to go back to the passengers and keep them calm."

"Shouldn't we just evacuate now?" Nasr asks, biting her lip.

"And go where, Nasr? We're still a long way from Crockett. We'd be waiting a long time for rescue."

"If anyone's coming to rescue us at all," Driscoll mutters.

Lira clenches her jaw. How can she save the goddamn crew if they won't save themselves?

"Enough," she warns, her voice low and level.

"Saints of sisterfucking shit," Nasr moans.

Where the hell is DeSouza? Nasr's not going to be any good with the passengers in her state. Lira stands, wobbling on her injured calf. The headache thankfully stays in the background, and her hands don't tremble too much.

"Belay that. I'll go talk to the passengers," she says. "Nasr, I want you to sweep B-Deck and make sure it's secure. Callum will join you after."

"If you're going down there, sir," Callum says, "you might want to head to the infirmary first. There's some pretty serious scrapes and bruises on A-Deck, and I think more than a couple passengers might need a sedative."

A familiar hunger gnaws her mind. There's plenty of stimbulbs in the infirmary too. In case she needs them.

"Good suggestion, Callum," Lira agrees.

Who will ever notice a few missing stimbulbs?

Callum and Driscoll unstrap Juarez's body from the bulkhead and take it away. Nasr stands at Driscoll's station, keeping an eye on things and off Erinn Juarez's body. Her eyes are red, but she's stopped crying. After, she heads for the exit hatch but stops and turns to Lira before she goes.

"She always wanted you to be captain when she was gone," Nasr says with an enigmatic smile. Lira starts. It's not the farewell she was expecting. She stands alone in the semi-silence of the bridge for several moments. In the pallid light of the comet, she ponders what else Juarez might have wanted.

There's a burst of static from the chirruping comms. Abe's baritone calls through.

"Lir."

Not *captain*, not *skipper*. Abe sounds serious. Whatever he and Mags found, it must be bad.

"What's our status? What does Mags say?"

Abe's voice catches like he's forgotten how to speak.

"Abe?"

It's rare for the bioengineer to be so at a loss for words.

"The whole engineering compartment is flooded with rotting biomass, Lira. I think the valves failed. I can't . . ."

"Can't what?" It's not like the engineer to hang on every word.

"Abe, come on. Talk to me."

Abe sighs through the comm. "I can't find Mags. Lir, you'd better just come see."

Lira folds her arms to keep her hands from a new bout of shaking. The passengers—and the stimbulbs—would have to wait.

Biomass is the lifeblood of a biotic vessel like the *Grass is Greener*. Synthesized from five different algal cultures and suspended in an artificial plasma, the fluid is pumped through all the organic systems of a starship, carrying not only nutrients but also commands from the rudimentary intelligence of the biotic core. It's a more primitive cousin of the blood that flows in a synthetic's veins. In a healthy vessel, biomass is a brilliant cyan with a faint bioluminescent glow and a clean, vegetal fragrance.

The engineering compartment is awash in spilled biomass, but the ship's blood is far from healthy. Black strands of dying biomass ooze from the crystal stems of broken conduits, filling the deck with a dank light the color of lead. An ammoniac reek stings Lira's eyes and nose. Underlying that is a whiff of rot and earth more appropriate to a Crockett storm cellar than the hold of a biotic vessel.

In the engine pit, the humps of the main engines crest the fetid pool like a pair of coffins washed up in a flood. Ropey tissues of congealing biomass clutch at the shrouded drives as if trying to pull them back under. The troubling image brings to mind the Oleander myths of sea monsters Abe likes to share in the dark of their bunk.

"Saints," Lira mutters.

"I've cleaned up plenty of spilled biomass in my time, Lir," Abe says behind her in the corridor, "but I've never seen anything like this."

She's not even sure where to begin the cleanup. The loss seems total.

"I'm afraid it's even worse than it looks," Abe says.

"How can it be worse?" She instantly regrets asking.

Worry gathers in cracks around Abe's usually jovial eyes. He shines a torch to the farthest reaches of the compartment where the vacuum pumps lie encrusted in biomass. "The evac pump's got a crack in the manifold. Not sure what would happen if I tried to pump all this out in the usual way."

He wrinkles his nose at the garbage smell wafting through the compartment.

Lira reconsiders stepping inside for another perspective. There's no telling what other solvents might be swirling in the murky depths of the biomass leak though, and there are some drive chemicals that can eat the rubber soles off deck boots.

"What the hell happened here? Containment pressure was nominal. We were hardly moving."

"Good question," Abe says. "If I could look at the plumbing more closely..."

He juts a thumb at the swampy mess.

"So we're dead in space," she confirms.

"I'm afraid so, Skipper," he nods sadly.

"Don't call me that."

Abe raises an eyebrow, surprised at her sudden pique.

"Skipper," she explains. "That was Juarez."

"Okay. How should I call you?" Abe frowns, realizing this is a continuation of their conversation in the sensor ladderwell.

Lira frowns, wondering why she brought it up now.

"Okay then, *Captain*," he says, deciding on the safest choice for now. "There's more."

Grimacing, Lira clings to the hatchway and leans in to look where the beam of his handlight is pointing. She puts small dents in the hatch frame with her grip.

The light beam rakes at a bit of debris bobbing at the surface of the sludge of biomass. It's a deck boot with thick soles, laces untied. There's a leg attached.

Sisterfucking saints.

Magnus Lin. The shaking comes back, and no amount of squeezing the hatch helps.

"It's not your fault, Lir."

Abe gently pulls her back from the door. Takes her hands in his own. Worry and sadness steal into his deep-set eyes. Anger flashes in Lira as she mistakes it for pity.

"Of course it isn't!" she snaps. She feels her usual composure fracture into a million shards of glass. This is not how she wants to respond, with frustration, with emotion. "But I plotted our jump," she fumes. "And our course around the navigational anomaly. I don't make errors like this, Abe. I *can't.*"

He nods, but he seems unsure. "The comet's uncharted. These are rough seas."

She yanks herself away from Abe, turning her gaze back on Mags's deck boot. "Our charts are out of date."

Abe shrugs, rubbing his thumb and forefinger together. "Juarez made the call not to budget for that this quarter."

"It was a foolish decision, and one I couldn't talk her out of. I thought I could take up the slack."

"You did your best," Abe sighs. "We all know it."

"You do, huh? And will you all say that?"

Say that to whatever civilian or corporate authorities will investigate this fiasco, she means.

"You did as the skipper ordered. We can *all* vouch for that. They'd need proof of malfeasance or negligence before they could charge you. A history of repeat offenses before they could even convene a hearing."

"Right," she says. *Exactly what I'm afraid of.*

She rubs her temples against the throbbing in her skull. The pulsing in her head matches the random clicks that echo in the comm system.

Clickclick-clickity. Throb. Throb.

Abe watches her, his expression like an engineer deciding how to fix a balky machine.

"I'm fine," she snaps, not liking that look.

"When's the last time you had a full diagnostic?" Abe blunders right into the sore point.

It's her turn to rub her fingers together in protest of Juarez's money woes.

"It's not an excuse. You're a member of this crew, not some piece of equipment."

Saints of shit, Abe is oblivious how thin the decking is. She flashes him a tight smile.

"You would know, yes?"

Abe colors.

"I might," he retorts.

"You have *no* idea, Abe. None."

Angry now, Abe crosses his arms. "What's all this about, Lira?" The air is thick between them, and it has little to do with the decaying biomass in engineering.

"Right now, Abe, I need you to be my bioengineer, not my lover. Not my friend. Can you?" She actually needs him to be all three, but it's more than she's up to processing.

"Sure," he mutters sulkily.

"Good," she says, softening her tone. He's lost friends today too. The moments stretch on, and she realizes he's waiting for her to say more. Time to concentrate on being his captain.

"You said you can't pump the compartment out in the 'usual way.' What do you have in mind, Abe?"

He grins, and though it's strained, he seems glad to be back on solid decking. "You won't like it, Captain."

"Tell me."

"Let's decompress the whole deck. We've got the main cargo airlocks nearby. It'll be like flushing a giant head."

"And coat the rest of B-Deck in all the shit," she warns. But it's not a bad idea.

"Maybe. But then at least I can get to the engines. Freeze off the punctured biomass flow. See if there's any way to salvage the mess."

"Nasr's already working on sealing off B-Deck," Lira says. That's doubly important now since the secondary passenger deck links somewhat directly with engineering. The last thing she wants is to blow any stray passengers out of the airlocks.

"She's looking for DeSouza too."

"She'll locate him, Lir," he says.

"I know," she says with another glance at Mags's boot. "I'm just afraid what she'll find when she does."

"Damn, Lir. And tomorrow was card night too." The deckhands and the engineers had a poker habit they fed once a week. Despite Abe's mentoring, Mags usually lost.

"He was a good kid. Lousy at cards but a great engineer. I should fish him out of there before I blow the deck."

"I know. But you can't be wading into that muck. I need you."

Abe nods. Despite everything, he knows her needs run deeper than a captain's.

"You'd better get up to the infirmary and get those medical supplies, Captain."

Lira feels a twinge of guilt for the permission he knowingly gives her.

A twinge of relief too.

The infirmary lies well aft of the central crew lift, damn near the stern of the ferry and almost as far from the B-Deck head as it's possible for Durance Pike to travel. He curses as he stumbles through the snaking passageways, steered less by the faded orientation guides printed on the bulkhead and more by the intangible bump of direction. A tug of duty—or desperation—pulling him along.

Staying on his feet is hard, every step a plodding referendum against Brother Hong's crusade. Maybe it's a test from the Nameless Ones, an evaluation of his worthiness. Pike assumes that he passes because before too long he stands at the infirmary door.

A swipe of the deckhand's keybadge admits him without fuss. The medical compartment is tiny, enough room for only a single examination table in the center of the cabin. Near a small desk with a built-in autolab is another door exiting toward the stern. Storage lockers line the bulkheads, but only the largest—a tall cabinet stretching from deck to overhead—is locked. A red light winks at Pike, beckoning him to the medical treasures inside. Roberto's badge opens that too.

Pike stands at the locker, swaying. A gray fog clouds the edge of his vision. Unseen ice freezes his hands, his feet. His lungs balk at drawing breath. He just leans on the exam table for a moment, focuses on breathing.

Roberto is already sitting there.

The young man, his eyes clouded and dull, smiles and waves. His fingers are smeared with blood, and his mousy hair is spiky with more.

"Hi, sir. I told you I'd get you to the infirmary," the deckhand chirps with a too-wide smile.

Startled, Pike lunges at him, pain strafing needles up his side. He bounces off the exam table and collapses instead back into the med locker, smearing an arc of blood on the deck. Wobbling on its central pillar, the table tilts to one side, empty. Roberto has vanished.

Saints of shit, now he's hallucinating?

"What are you doing, Rance?" asks Brother Hong.

His mentor, friend, and lover leans against the bulkhead near the locker. He's wearing the full gray robes of the temple ritual, complete with the heavy bronzium chest plate he inscribed with the supposed biotic symbols of the Nameless Ones.

"Trying to get . . . that sisterfucker." He points to the deckhand that's no longer there. *Was never there,* he tells himself.

Brother Hong blinks. His brown eyes are warm.

"He should be dead," Pike explains.

"So should you, my friend," Brother Hong replies with a sad smile.

"Not. Going anywhere. Yet," Pike replies through gritted teeth. It's more to himself since the odds Brother Hong has appeared in the infirmary to castigate him are extremely fucking low. He claws his way up from the deck, using the locker door as a crutch. Inside the cabinet, little vials and medbulbs tinkle and clatter with the promise of healing.

"You ain't really here, Brother," he says.

The priest of the Gray Temple shakes his head in agreement.

"Figured."

Pike glances at his hands. His fingertips are tipped in bilious caps of gangrene and stiff with cold. He fumbles through the vials looking for the painkillers.

"So you got any advice, or you just going to stand there and heap scorn on me, Markos," he tells the apparition when it doesn't vanish.

Markos. Brother Hong always called him Rance but never reciprocated the intimacy of his own given name. In his presence, Pike would never have dared to use it, but now was different. This is as close as he'll probably ever be to the man again.

"The pain is a gift," Markos explains.

"Yeah. From that fucking. Engineer."

Markos comes and stands right behind Pike. It makes him uneasy, the apparition standing so close. Stirs up feelings that aren't helpful. Pike distracts himself by holding up an auto injector of morphine in his blackened hands.

"And also from the seed that you planted in the engineering compartment," Markos whispers in his ear.

Pike gets chills. *The spore.* Another instant of lucidity, and it sounds ridiculous, a fairy tale from a rabid idealist. Then Pike remembers he's one of those too.

"I did it for you," he admits to the Markos apparition. Pike's stomach flip-flops like he's given a present to a new crush. Dammit, he's an old man, and Markos Hong left him a long time ago.

"I'm grateful. It grows, Rance. Inside the ship. It's taken full root in the rich soil of your faithful body." Pike imagines Markos running a finger down his neck. He wheels on the monk, the auto injector momentarily forgotten in the white-cold heat of his agony.

"It. Sisterfucking hurts, Markos!" He means more than the wound.

Markos gives a small shrug and smiles.

"This what you planned all along, ain't it?" Pike accuses, poking Markos in the chest.

"Who can say? I'm not really here."

Pike snarls and jams the injector into the crook of his left arm. The device hisses, and within seconds, a tingling warmth spreads along his arm and into his body, melting the icy grip of the void. For the first time since leaving engineering, the clouds in Pike's mind truly clear.

Markos, of course, is gone, vanished into the same ether as Roberto the deckhand.

The hallucinations of a dying man, Pike tells himself. But isn't the phantom Markos telling the truth?

Was their all-too-brief love affair merely a ploy to eventually *transform* him with the spore? Maybe it was just something bad in the ferry's old biomass, an infection spread in his open wound. A bout of dizziness sways him, and Pike is certain the fever hasn't left him despite the drugs.

He injects himself with another painkiller and a stimbulb for good measure. Colors sharpen. In the cold light of the infirmary, the shadows of his mind recede.

The locker door swings by its hinges. Broken vials and plastic tabs crunch underfoot. Blood paints the examination table, the locker. It's his of course. The ship's comm buzzes and crackles as if full of bees. Though he's staved it off, the light of the comet still presses against his consciousness.

The drugs can only help so much. Even so, he counts out five more auto injectors of painkillers. It ought to be enough.

He shrugs out of his ruined duster. His shirt's soaked through with gore, and more of the little green-black puffs waft out from the sucking tear. He wipes the wound with the coat and nearly passes out. He injects himself with all five vials. His mind dulls a bit, though the pain recedes.

Pike finds some sprayflesh and empties the whole cartridge into the wound. It stops the bleeding finally. Little flecks of green stud the hardening surface of the biotic skin.

Better.

He dons his coat again. Fills his pockets with more sprayflesh and stimbulbs. Another stimbulb finally levels out the pain with clearer thoughts. A medical scalpel makes an adequate replacement for the knife he lost in engineering.

Pike contemplates his shrinking options. At present, the ship seems to be on course for the comet. He can hide somewhere up here, ride the ferry all the way into the comet for whatever destiny awaits him in the light of the Nameless Ones.

But Pike doubts the crew will let the ferry continue to drift into the comet's grasp. He's certainly in no condition to hunt them down either. He's been lucky so far, but injured and weaponless are not advantages.

No doubt there are lifepods or EVA suits he could don. Floating to the comet on his own seems daunting but achievable at least. That look in Roberto's eyes though. And the reaction of some of the passengers. They could feel the same things he was feeling. It wouldn't be fair to deprive them of union with the Nameless Ones.

Would it?

Airlock. There's one back through the aft door somewhere. He'd seen it marked on a schematic in the passageways here. At the very least, he can hide out on the exterior of the ferry while the crew searches in vain. Sabotage sensor vanes or maneuvering thrusters.

With what, Rance? A more lucid part of his mind asks.

Toward the fore door comes the whirr and thunk of the central crew lift.

The air murmurs around him, flavored with the scent of advanced plastics and neurocarbon biotic fibers. Pike doesn't have time to consider how he can detect those before his blood runs cold.

A *synthetic*?

Outside the infirmary is a rustling as the synthetic fumbles with a keybadge. Pike slips to the rear door. His plan is solid. There's not much ship left for him to retreat to, but it's a bad idea to face off with a synthetic until you know you have a decided advantage. Most synthetics are tough sisterfuckers, but the combat models can twist your head off easy as unscrewing a jar of salted eggs.

The rear door leads Pike into a maze of life support systems—heat exchangers bundled in thermal batting and blue-green conduits of biomass bubbling along. He pauses at one of the inflow tubes, studying the pulsing goop flowing past. Gossamer black filaments thread through the healthy tissue. It won't be long.

So the ferry is infected too. Phantom Markos was telling the truth. A thrill shudders through him. It's real.

And the ship is on my side, he realizes. *It wants to meet the Nameless Ones too.* Pike wonders whether its biotic systems perceived the comet's call. If it felt as conflicted about it as he did.

A shadow appears in the port of the infirmary door. Pike tucks himself behind a lattice of conduits, peering through the distorted lens of a crystal vein.

The door slides open. A slight woman in a crew uniform marked with navigator's pips limps out into the corridor from the infirmary. She appears human, her skin of burnished copper and short brown hair that echoes the regulation cut on a tighter ship. A handsome and strong-looking woman. Her eyes give her away though. They are a brilliant, luminescent gold, and they shine in the semi-darkness of the passageway like a cat's in the dark.

A loosely wrapped bandage, stiff with dried fluid, dangles from her calf. And wounded, no less. Definitely an advantage Pike can use.

Pike holds his breath, tensing for the fight. He squeezes the handle of the scalpel tight. Synthetics, for all their strength, still have weak spots. They were still mostly flesh and blood, of a sort. The processor ganglia at the base of the neck, for example, are vulnerable to a sharp blade. He has stealth on his side, and her wound too. If the synthetic isn't an armored combat model, Pike just might have a chance.

"DeSouza?" The synthetic's voice is a Core-accented contralto. Komeda

Intelligence Systems or possibly Gamma AI. He recalls both companies produce combat models too.

The synthetic peers around but fails to spot him. She never comes into the passageway, remaining just inside the infirmary, her hands shaking on the frame.

Fear? It's an odd trait for a synthetic. Discretion then. Caution definitely. Self-preservation is important to any lifeform. Pike's chest burns from holding his breath for so long. The strange, artificial scent of the synthetic's chemical sweat fills his nostrils. Pike dares a slow, controlled exhalation.

Patience, Rance. This ain't the first time you've done an ambush.

Strange how the voice sounds a bit like his mama's. His fingers are numb; he's gripping the scalpel so hard.

The synthetic finally retreats back into the infirmary for good, sealing the lock on the door as she goes. Her shadow moves away from the viewport.

Durance Pike breathes out and inhales deeply. Another shot of painkiller chases away the resulting agony.

A wounded and frightened synthetic in charge of a ship with seventy-five passengers, some of them dazed by the comet's light, and a dwindling and sloppy crew. Now those are the kind of advantages an experienced killer like himself can work with.

Lira shakes in the wreckage of the infirmary, clutching DeSouza's keybadge in her fist. She'd found it under a pile of crushed stimbulbs that had spilled from a locker. The whole damn infirmary is streaked with blood. DeSouza's? Little green-white puffs like mold collect on the drying blood, and Lira can't help but think of the nightmare in engineering.

The comm panel blinks at her from the autolab desk. She should call this in to Abe right away, or even Driscoll, but instead she counts the still-intact stimbulbs rolling across the deck. Fourteen. Their whole supply. She rests her throbbing head in her hands.

With all the blood he's lost, DeSouza can't go too far.

Why go anywhere at all?

Lira scoops a handful of the stimbulbs from the deck. She presses one into the crook of her arm, and the injector sighs, pushing back the fatigue with the chemical lift.

With her mind a little clearer, Lira turns her attention to the door that leads back to life support. There'd been no sign of DeSouza back there, but he might have stumbled all the way back to the stern airlock.

Somehow, that thought disquiets her, though she can't say why. In a confused and injured state, might he accidentally open a pressure door, thinking he was heading back to the bridge? It seems unlikely he'd make that sort of error.

Maybe as improbably that a synthetic navigator—a stimbulb addict and the killer of a thousand people—would doom another ship.

Sisssshhhhh.

Another stimbulb throws a chemical blanket over those useless ruminations. The cocktail of metabolic boosters is having a diminished effect on Lira's biotic systems with every injection, but it's still enough to dull the growing apprehension. She can indulge when their boots sink into the soil on Silas's Crossing.

The comm unit sputters. The static crackles through the speakers in regular patterns like *Grass is Greener* itself is trying to tell her something.

Does the ship want me to go back into life support or back to the bridge? A tingle shudders through her backbone. A warning or confirmation? Both?

Lira scowls. Why should she be apprehensive about searching for DeSouza? The kid no doubt needed the medical attention Lira was rated to provide.

What if it's not DeSouza back there?

What a curious thought. If not DeSouza, then who? An injured passenger, straying from A-Deck before Nasr secured all the hatches? They might have found DeSouza's badge and headed for the infirmary. That still begs the question—where is her deckhand if not up here?

Images from the passenger deck security feed flicker through her precise memory. What of that rangy, old salt in the black duster, hurrying from the lavatory, clutching his bag like a man possessed? Lira's skin crawls as she remembers the intense look of concentration—or pain—on the man's face.

Oh, saints of shit. Could that bastard have gotten all the way up here?

Lira steels herself, expecting the old man to appear through the life support door any second. She's no combat model but could most likely handle him.

Her wounded calf aching, she limps to the autolab's comm and keys in an override on the door just to be sure. The door chimes a minor key, letting her know it's sealed. Letting anyone on the other side know too.

She leans over the comm. It's judicious to call for backup.

"Abe, this is Lira. Come in." *Keep your voice steady, Lira. Just in case he's listening.*

"This is Mistri," Abe says at once. He's hard to hear with the interference in the comms. Lira doesn't dare boost the gain though in case someone on the other side of the door is listening.

"Have we found DeSouza yet?"

"No, not yet." He sounds dejected.

"Have Nasr look in the out-of-order lavatory on B-Deck. Send Callum to help."

"They didn't find anything," he pauses. "I'm about to depressurize the whole deck."

"Have them check one more time."

"Okay, Captain."

Lira takes a deep breath, filling her biotic lungs. "Before you evacuate the deck, Abe, I want you to meet me in the security locker."

"Weapons?" He sounds incredulous.

"Yes."

"Okay."

On a ship like this, there's little call for weapons, but for rare acts of piracy or disruptive passengers, Juarez always maintained it never hurt to be prepared. The tiny security locker just below the bridge contains three stun rifles, two needler pistols, and two sets of shock batons.

In all Lira's years serving aboard *Grass is Greener*, the only time Juarez ever ordered the locker opened was for maintenance and inspection. She let a lot of things slide on the ferry, but that wasn't one of them. Lira always wonders whether the skipper kept the weapons charged on account of her. Had Juarez expected an inevitable betrayal of her indentured synthetic? She needn't have worried.

On her way out of the infirmary, Lira pauses once more at the med locker. There's a field kit with a sturdy shoulder strap. She loads it up with auto injectors, sprayflesh, and plenty of stimbulbs.

As Juarez said, never hurts to be prepared.

The passageways of life support circle Pike around a funhouse of pulsing conduits, the silver drums of oxygen exchangers, and their distended biotic air sacs. His careful plans unravel with his mind, drifting on fevered gray winds across a barren plain. Things had been so clear before.

Find the stern airlock. Escape across the hull. Enter engineering after the crew decompressed the deck.

Pike lurches off the bulkheads, trying but failing to find that airlock. Despite the pharmacopeia of meds he'd injected, his thoughts are fogging up, filling with a greasy light. His hands itch like a sisterfucking saint, and the scalpel is lost somewhere in the maze. His arms are pathways for a billion unseen ants—and his belly, where the engineer skewered him, the heart of their squirming nest. He shrugs out of his duster, bringing new flavors of agony without name. His skin wants to slough off too, spilling his red secret self all over the filthy deck of the old ferry.

The spore's inky stains have crept up his arms, spotting his sun-ripened skin in gangrenous hues. He's infected like the ship. Waking.

You and the ship, waking together. Like all disciples of Brother Hong, Rance.

He tells himself it's still what he wants. To greet the Nameless Ones after long eons of sleep, to make Brother Hong proud. It's the only thought that brings stillness to his mind. Except for—

Mama.

Pike lurches to a stop before a junction of conduits, maybe the same one he'd hidden behind minutes before. Tarry biomass pulses through the ferry's crystalline veins. He imagines he hears Mama's wavering voice calling out over the plains.

Blood. DeSouza. Decompress. Weapons.

The words abrade his ears like plugs of steel wool. It's the synthetic, not Mama who's speaking. There's no comm nearby though. How can he hear her?

A monofilament wire of lucidity sears through Pike's brain.

The ship *can hear her.*

He and the ship share a fate after all. They are both called to arms in Brother Hong's tireless crusade. In Pike's haste to welcome the Nameless Ones on Brother Hong's behalf, he hasn't even considered reaching out to *Grass is*

Greener for aid. Maybe the ship hasn't thought to ask *him* either. The cores of biotic vessels are crude, warp-seeking instincts. It might not even know he's there.

But if Pike could reach out somehow, let *Grass is Greener* know that they both want the same thing?

Then they might be unstoppable.

As Lira fears, they find Roberto DeSouza dead in a stall on B-Deck's aft lavatory. Callum, assisting Nasr with the search, was the one to find him. She calls Lira before the captain can make it to the security locker. Abe joins her and Callum in the lavatory, and the three of them stand over poor DeSouza's crumpled body. The back of his head is cracked open and studded with shards of broken mirror. The probability that he'd been thrown into the mirror and then into the stall by the ship's erratic movement alone was exceedingly small.

There is a lot of blood too. Inconsistent with just DeSouza's wounds and more in keeping with the trail of blood Lira'd found in the infirmary.

"Saints of shit," the blonde deckhand exclaims for the third time in as many minutes.

Lira nudges in next to Callum, peering into the stall. A satchel of cheap brocade, like the kind you find in the tourist alleys of the central city sprawls of Silas's Crossing, is wadded up under Roberto's head. The bag is empty save for a curious black sand. She's careful not to touch it.

Lira resists the urge to pull out a stimbulb from her medkit. While Abe knows about her frequent use, Callum does not, and there's no reason to give her deckhand cause for concern now. Lira's grateful the headache hasn't gotten worse, but the tremors in her hands are escalating.

Callum doesn't notice, and her big blue eyes shimmer, her only concession to grief. Lira recalls she and DeSouza slept around some but less seriously than Lira and Abe. Save Lira and Driscoll, there was almost no coupling on this ship that had not been tried. The flings usually didn't last though. They all spent too much time together just working.

Abe clenches his jaw, no doubt thinking again of the off-hour poker games in engineering with Callum, Magnus, and DeSouza. DeSouza, unlike Mags, almost always won, though he was never an ass about it.

"That's not DeSouza's bag, Captain. Someone else was in here," Callum says through her angry tears.

"I believe we have a killer aboard," Lira says. "And possibly a saboteur, though his motives remain opaque."

Abe looks up sharply from tending DeSouza's body.

"Lir—" he begins.

"I bet it was that asshole in the black duster," Callum sneers.

Ice water jets through Lira's veins. That guy on the holocam?

"What do you know about him?" Lira demands.

Callum squints her eyes at Lira, angry the guy had got past her.

"Didn't think much of him honestly," Callum says. "The old sweaty boarded at Silas's Crossing. Skin like a leather bag, and a permanent stoop. I marked him as a yokel from Crockett. He glared at me like he knew what I was thinking."

"He's more than just a yokel," Lira warns. "He's managed to kill three members of the crew and perhaps fatally wounded *Grass is Greener*."

"Fatally?" Callum squeaks.

Lira looks away, wishing to retract her assessment. As a navigator, she is accustomed to speaking frankly to the crew. A captain must practice greater discretion.

"Check the manifest," Abe grunts, eager to change the subject.

Callum digs out a logpad from her suit pocket. Her brow furrows as she searches. "Seat R37P. Pike. Durance Pike. Bought a ticket on Silas's Crossing. One way."

"*One way*," Abe echoes.

"He might have been just returning home," Lira says, "but obviously something changed."

"The comet," Callum says.

A tingle runs up Lira's spine. She can't disagree. From the moment it appeared on her scopes, events had proceeded toward entropy.

"We need to arm ourselves, Skipper," Callum says, eyes fierce.

"Abe and I have already conferred on that point," Lira nods. "We'll get weapons from the locker. Callum, I want you to go back to Nasr on A-Deck."

Callum shakes her head. "Like hell. Not without a stunner. What if this sweaty comes at me?"

"I don't believe Pike will return to the passenger decks."

Callum shakes her head in disbelief. "How can you know that?"

Lira gestures to the bloody stall. "Pike's lost a lot of blood. I found the same patterns splashed all over the infirmary. And DeSouza's badge as well. I sealed him in life support."

"Life support?" Callum shrieks. "What if he figures out how to suffocate us all?"

Lira raises a mollifying hand. "I'll shoot him first," she says. "Now, go back to A-Deck and prep the passengers for possible evacuation."

"Some of the passengers are acting odd too, Captain. They just sit and stare out the viewport at that thing." Callum suppresses a shudder.

Lira sighs. There aren't enough crew to handle every passenger turning into a Durance Pike.

"Keep it quiet, Kate. Don't tell Nasr until Abe or I bring up the weapons."

Callum nods sullenly and departs to the cavernous and empty B-Deck.

Lira drags Abe right behind, making a beeline for the security locker. She bypasses the main passageways, sticking to the ladderwells and maintenance junctions. If Pike's managed to find his way past the locked infirmary doors, she'd rather not face him without a stunner in her hands. Abe stops at a ventilation screen, scowling. Thin black runnels of infected biomass drip down the scruffy wall, pooling on the deck. Just like engineering.

"Saints of shit, Lira," he says sadly. "What did that sisterfucker do to my ship?"

He runs a finger through the ooze and sniffs. His face wrinkles at the strong reek of ammonia.

"I intend to ask him, Abe," she says, sounding more resolute than she feels. She pulls him away from the contaminated vent. After they neutralize Pike, they can evaluate the ferry's condition. If an evacuation is inevitable—

But Lira's not ready to make that decision yet, not while there's still time.

"Abe, come on," she says when he slows at another infected conduit junction, slack-jawed.

The engineer acquiesces, stumbling along. He wipes biomass from his fingers, leaving streaks of green and black on the thigh of his jumpsuit. Lira hopes the infection isn't contagious.

The air in the security locker is dense, almost humid. Just entering the codes on the weapon cabinets is enough to make Lira and Abe sweat. Some of the sweating can be attributed to tension, Lira knows, but she's detected an average three-degree temperature rise in the last fifteen minutes. Thirty-two degrees and still climbing.

The heat only intensifies her headache. She uses stimbulbs openly in front of Abe now. He watches her inject two as they pull out the first of the rifles. He clenches his jaw and says nothing. He needs her to be focused.

The security locker is located just below the bridge, between the two thick bulkheads that undergird the entire command section. An excellent heat trap. What the designers of the J-6 Type ferry had originally placed there is lost to memory and six decades of modifications. As its latest owner, Juarez had decided the narrow space was well suited to storing weapons.

Lira had argued with Juarez over the wisdom of putting firearms beneath a critical location such as the bridge. The skipper waved off her concerns—only stocking stunners and needlers. Nothing explosive.

"Besides," she'd said, "wouldn't you want them handy if you needed them?"

Despite the stifling heat, there's a permanent chill settling between her shoulder blades. Somewhere, straight aft of them, Durance Pike lurks, bleeding in the dark. She's had Driscoll lock life support down with overrides from the bridge, but it's a dangerous place to have him trapped.

"Why did he attack us?" Lira wonders, discarding a spent stimbulb in the medical kit. She adjusts its strap, resisting the temptation to grab another dose.

"Saints of shit, who knows," Abe says roughly. He won't meet her eyes. "Maybe Lin and DeSouza surprised him in the act."

"The act of what?"

Abe doesn't have an answer. They gather the weapons as the wall comm clicks and warbles as if there's a flock of birds inside. The sound still buzzes in her head, but she no longer thinks it's all in her aural nodes. Abe hears it too. He gives the comm a sour look. *Grass is Greener* is dying somehow, thanks to whatever bomb Durance Pike set off in engineering. Lira's no longer certain they can save the ferry. But maybe she can still save the passengers. The crew.

Abe passes her a stunner rifle. It's rated to overload a human nervous system and will even give a synthetic one a hell of a jolt. Lira feels an unproductive moment of savagery, wishing the stunner could deliver a fatal shock. Pike has many lives to answer for.

For himself, Abe chooses a needler. The sleek pistol shoots micro darts filled with a powerful sedative. He clips the gun to his toolbelt where it will be easy to draw should Pike appear. Lira doesn't plan to wait for Pike to leap from the shadows like a boogeyman in a nightmare holo. She's already made her decision.

"I'm going after him," she announces to Abe.

"Not alone, Lir," he shakes his head. Though he tries to sound matter of fact about it, there's an unmistakable note of rising panic in his voice.

"I'll be fine, Abe. I need you in engineering, trying to get the engines started. Or deciding they can't be."

"While you go hunt a killer in the dark? You may be synthetic, Lira, but he can still kill you."

He twists his mouth, the words seemingly tasting sour, but she doesn't respond.

She's brooded on deactivation and death every day since the *Highline*, but she'd never really faced it aboard *Grass is Greener*. She considers that she might die today, and the realization leaves her feeling hollow.

Abe slings another stunner over his shoulder. He chews on the inside of his cheek, deciding whether to risk pushing his way through Lira's silence.

"I have to go after him, Abe," she finally says. "I'm the only member of the crew who can."

Abe looks at her, anger glinting in his eyes.

"You're not the expendable one, Lira. You're our captain—and our navigator."

"In theory," she admits.

The anger he'd been trying to bottle up finally explodes.

"What the hell does that mean?"

I still hide the truth from him, she reflects sadly. She's protecting a secret that may not even matter in a few hours anyway. Perhaps it never really mattered at all.

Lira lays a hand on his arm. He ceases fiddling with the weapons.

"It means that eleven years ago, before *Grass is Greener*, Juarez and I served on a deep space refinery for HYL. As lovers, we weren't compatible, but we became close friends. I was assigned to the nav crew, a junior liaison to the biotic core of that ship. Juarez was third mate, one of the pilots.

"We served on that vessel for five years until the day we shunted out of warp with a load of heavy metals bound for the manufacturing facility in the Adamson asteroid belt. Our ship was the *Highline*."

Abe's eyes go wide. Every spacer knows about the *Highline* incident—one of the worst industrial accidents of the last fifty years. He opens his mouth to reply, but this time he's truly speechless.

"It was my calculation error that caused us to shunt from warp prematurely."

"Oh, saints of shit, Lir." Abe chokes on his words. All the anger's drained out of him, replaced by shock.

"Juarez wasn't on duty when *Highline* emerged from warp space," she continues, "But I was. I'd brought us out only thirty thousand kilometers from the facility instead of three hundred thousand, and the drives were still running full bore from our reversion to real space.

"The captain swung us around to brake, but *Highline* wasn't a dancer, and we got caught up in our own spacetime wake. The maneuver nearly cracked the ship in half. And while we dumped 98 percent of our fuel in the deceleration burn, it didn't slow us enough. Captain Ramee gave the order to abandon ship, but all the bridge officers stayed, determined to save it. All except me.

"I was . . . afraid. So I ran for the lifepods."

The moaning comm lends an eerie chord to the silence. Lira hurries to fill the quiet, lest Abe's shock harden into something worse.

"Juarez was in her bunk at the time of the accident, but when the evacuation order was given, she was one of the first to the lifepods. She found me cowering between the bulkheads, disoriented and confused. I'd never been so incapacitated by fear, Abe. She shoved me into one of the lifepods before the *Highline* collided with Adamson A621 at near reversion velocity. As we boosted away, I confessed the accident had been my fault. She said nothing and piloted us away from the expanding fireball.

"She lied in the inquests that followed. She told the investigators that I was with her at the time of the accident. Because of our past dalliances, the falsehood wasn't questioned."

"I knew," Abe sighs. "Or I suspected something like that. Most of the *Highline* records are sealed, but I snooped around when Juarez bought the *Grass is Greener*. Wanted to see what sort of person my new commanders were. It was obvious there was an incident in the past, but her references were stellar.

"I wish you'd told me though, Lira."

And of course, she should have. But their relationship had always been mostly about sex. Only recently had she entertained the idea of a deeper connection. And while Juarez had kept her secret, she had also kept the skipper's. If word ever got out that she'd lied at the inquest, then it meant the end of both their careers—or worse.

"I couldn't, Abe. The skipper and I kept each other's secret. She got settlement money and bought a ship. I got a job and avoided probable deactivation."

"Hell, Lira. What can I say?"

"You can tell me that *Grass is Greener* isn't *Highline*. That the pseudo-comet out there isn't Adamson A621."

Abe flushes. "Actually, I meant what can I say about Erinn," he explains. "It's unconscionable she held that over you for over a decade."

"I held it over her too, Abe. But as the margins got thinner, I think she began to resent the expense of her synthetic navigator. Stimbulbs are a cheaper if less effective substitute for regular biotic maintenance."

"I could have helped," he sighs, his eyes like beads of glass.

"But then I doubt I could have tolerated you as a lover. Better to have stayed away from your bioengineer's tools."

His response is a frustrated grunt.

She examines one of the stun batons. The black rod delivers a bigger shock than the rifle, but she'd have to get too close to use it. Lira decides against slipping it into her belt loop. One more weapon he could take from her during a fight.

"I abandoned *Highline,* Abe. I ran, and a thousand people died. I'm sure as hell not going to abandon *Grass is Greener.*" She gives Abe one of the batons along with a meaningful look.

"Lir, I'm afraid we might have to. I've been serving aboard for two decades, and I've never seen *Grass is Greener* hurting so bad." He gestures to a ventilation screen and the inky biomass bubbling out from the slats. His brown eyes mist over with grief.

"The ship's sick. Infected by whatever Pike did. We should decompress the deck on the port side. Then Driscoll fires the thrusters on the same side to push us further away from the comet. Then we launch the lifepods. Hope Crockett Control's already sent a rescue ship."

Lira frowns. She trusts his assessment of the ferry's condition, but it's rare for him to exhibit such despondency.

"What if they haven't, Abe? What if the lifepods get caught in the grip of that comet? Don't we owe it to the passengers to try?"

Abe shrugs, but Lira can't tell whether he agrees or whether he's just given up.

It's a simple thing to imagine talking to the ship, Durance Pike thinks, *to tell it they can end their pain together. But it's another matter entirely to reckon out how.* Only minutes before, with another sprayskin patch freshly applied, painkillers coursing through his papery veins, Pike had thought all he must do is reach about and tell the ship he was there.

"I am here!" he screams, but if the ship can hear him, it doesn't reply. He finds himself wandering in circles through life support once more, the fog of torment rolling in. *Saints of shit, where's the goddamn airlock?*

Perhaps the ship is testing his resolve, the same way Brother Hong used to do. Maybe the ship's belief already outstrips his own.

No!

Didn't Pike see the comet first? Didn't he plant the spore into the ferry's beating heart? He awakened the ship, and not the other way 'round.

So let's save each other, goddammit.

He stands in front of the hatch to the airlock, panting. Pike grins. Maybe the ship does hear him! But the lock glows red, and the ship doesn't respond to his verbal commands.

No doubt, the captain's locked him out. With the stumps of his fat, unfeeling fingers, Pike presses the lock to no avail. The door requires a badge, and he'd lost Roberto's somewhere back in the infirmary. He could try smashing the delicate biotic components around him, but it might turn the ship against him when he most wants its cooperation.

"Okay, ship, let's do this together," he croaks, looking into the camera eye set into the comm unit. The speaker squawks and hisses. Assent? Or stubbornness?

Let's play it your way then.

Next to the airlock hatch is a DNA spiral of carbon mesh and steel-glass. A major biomass conduit—its contents still a dim, healthy cyan—runs from the deck to an air sac overhead. A flow pump divides the conduit in two, and there's a port for testing oxygenation of the biotic lung.

Pike doesn't have the tools for running that kind of diagnostic, but he and the ship do share something in common.

He stares at the blackening digits of his hand, studying the green veins that newly sprout from his fingertips and coil in tight bands around his fingers. They remind him of the haptic cilia wired into standard spacesuits and industrial loaders, the synthetic nerve fibers that connect an operator with their machine. Maybe he can get through to the ship, but he'll have to carve away a pound of flesh first.

Pike opens the port to the flow pump, and its liquid pulse grows louder. The opening is just big enough for his hand.

He hesitates, feeling a sudden electric jolt for what he's about to do. If it works, then in a short time, he will finally greet the Nameless Ones. He'll spread the news of Brother Hong's faithfulness and help usher in a new era. If it doesn't, he'll likely die screaming, his final charge unfulfilled.

You promised me I was meant for more than killing, Brother. I pray you're right.

Pike plunges his right arm into the port, burying it up to the elbow. The biomass plasma inside the filter is blood-warm. The substance coagulates on his fingers, and the gritty paste makes his palms tingle. The tendrils at the tips of his fingers sway in the biomass, tasting the rot in the lifeblood of the ship.

What do you think, ship? Pike asks. *Shall we go to the comet together?*

A surge of electricity erupts along his outstretched arm. A gray fog descends. He scrabbles against the diagnostic junction in a vain effort to keep his footing. Images roil in his semi-conscious vision. Corridors, deep within the ship. The B-Deck lavatory with the synthetic captain and her crew leaning over the deckhand he'd killed. The rest of the passengers, crowded into the forward section of A-Deck, staring at the comet, terror written in their wide, livestock eyes. The deeps beneath the engineering compartment where the biotic heart of the ship roils with the same desire to bask in the light of the Nameless Ones as him.

And there—the hatch to the airlock next to him and the hunched mountain of his quaking back as seen through the camera eye.

Open.

But the command isn't enough. The waking ship demands something of him now. A sacrifice of self to seal the communion begun in engineering.

His fingers brush the powerful suction of the flow turbine, and he knows what is required. Grunting, Pike forces his arm further into the port, grating his tingling hand along the razored tines of the turbine. His arm grows rigid, but surpassingly, he doesn't feel anything as the turbine chops his hand into mincemeat. So Pike pushes harder. The conduits run black and green and red. And still, he pushes harder. The blades nibble at his wrist.

Open the goddamn door.

Images again of all the decks—*thump*—and of engineering—*thump*—and of the ferry hanging stricken in space as the scarred bulk of the comet rolls and pulses below. *Thump.*

A constellation of debris fans out behind the strange comet. Rocks, dust, gas, bits of cosmic scrap caught in its inevitable gravitational wake. *Ships too.*

At last, Pike sees them for what they are, hanging motionless in the shadows of the vast cosmic body. Old freighters with fuel tanks so swollen with infected biomass the skins of their hulls have split apart like rotten fruit. An ancient cruise ship drifts, prow up, its portholes clogged and trailing motes that glint green and black—a million, billion star spores for Brother Hong to harvest. He sees a stray frigate too, its blasted hulk still bristling with long dead weapons and ancient forests of vacuum-hardened biomass. The cancerous eruptions resemble Brother Hong's tales of the spires of the temples of the Nameless Ones.

In the wan light of the arcing gases, Pike glimpses the true surface of the "comet"—a vista of jagged spires not of ice but of alien biomass, a living skin of warp space, roiling with vast, serpentine hulks and impossible geometries of writhing flesh.

Grass is Greener aches with desire to join the revel and, like the other vessels, to cavort forever in ecstatic orbits of the Nameless One's comet. Every centiliter of biomass quivers with this wanting, with the salvation and liberation that Pike can grant. But he must get to the engines first. He must show *Grass is Greener* the way.

The bones of his wrist grind into the blades of the turbine, and Pike is hurled from the port by newly bright, searing agonies. Where his hand had been, only a raw red stump remains. But even as he watches, the insidious green and black of the spore's growth mottles over the wound, sealing it, burning it.

Pike's screams are beyond sound.

Mama! He cries for comfort that's long since gone.

The lock to the airlock hatch turns green.

"Captain, I'm ready to evacuate B-Deck. Driscoll's a go on the port thrusters as soon as you give the word."

Abe's voice is barely audible through the static wailing through the comms, but Lira replies, "Affirmative." Not for the first time, she wonders if the ferry's failing organic systems will hold out much longer. She should give the order to launch the lifepods, but Callum said some of the passengers wouldn't go. Something held them to their seats.

On her way aft, she pauses in the crew galley for another stimbulb. Her satchel is almost empty, but she'll pass the infirmary on the way back to life support. That calms her shaking until she sees the autochef in the galley oozing the green-black lather of infected biomass.

The wound on her calf has barely healed, and Lira doesn't want to risk contamination. She's careful to step around the malfunctioning machine. If the crew deck is infected, then A-Deck probably is too. Maybe those passengers. She sends a comm to Abe to make sure that Nasr and Callum are armed. She can't hear his reply.

Saints of shit.

When the infirmary door slides open, she's engulfed in a blast of warm, humid air. Biomass rains from broken conduits in the overhead. The deck sloshes with a stinking film of contamination two inches thick. Pike must have sabotaged one of the junctions in life support.

The rest of her prized stimbulbs are adrift, tossed and swirled on the miniature pond. If not broken outright. *Shit.* The tremors start immediately.

"Pike!"

Her shouts are muffled by the contamination. A sound like ripping fabric blasts from the comms in response. Was the bridge trying to raise her or just a burst of random sound?

"Abe? Abe? Driscoll?"

Grass is Greener is dying. She's lost the ship, lost her crew. Lost herself. Lira steadies herself at the door. No. Those are irrational conclusions. She must focus if she's going to stop Pike.

And I'll have to wade through the sludge, she realizes. Whatever contaminates the biomass, she hopes it won't infect her. Her biotic components are a century more advanced than the ferry's. But her injured calf still burns, a reminder that the risk is real.

A jolt passes through the ship. Driscoll's firing the thrusters. *He was supposed to wait until after Abe decompressed B-Deck!*

She slams the heel of her hand against the infirmary lock, but the door stubbornly refuses to close. Another shudder passes through the deck, and standing waves rise on the infected sludge. It sloshes over Lira's boots. She has just enough time to brace herself against the bulkhead again before the ship lurches farther to starboard.

That's Abe decompressing B-Deck.

The extra acceleration throws Lira to the floor into the infected biomass. Her rifle is torn from her hands, and the stunner vanishes down the corridor on a stinking wave of slime. A deep, forlorn groan vibrates out of the hull. The infection and sudden acceleration is tearing it apart. Lira gasps, struggling to right herself in the slippery mess. Everything shakes. Her hands, her body. Her ship.

Under the bandage, the nerves of her injured calf catch fire. Somehow, she grabs hold of the grill of a fire suppression vent and hauls herself out of the muck. The flood subsides, and the shaking stops.

Something wails on the comms. Beneath the noise, though, she hears Abe's triumphant laugh.

"We did it, Captain! We're pulling away!"

Lira hangs from the wall, panting. *We did it. They did it.*

Now what do I do next?

Lira wonders if biomass will infect her through her dripping bandage, and if it does, how long she has. She draws the needler from the clip at her belt. *Long enough to stop Pike at least,* she promises herself.

Beneath the thin patch of sprayskin, Durance Pike's soul splits open like a rotten balloon.

It *erupts.*

A bulging fibroid of green-black tissue protrudes from the wound, seeping thick blood and oily biomass. To Pike's surprise, his transformation doesn't hurt. He writhes on the deck in a fog of joyless ecstasy. Burst conduits shower him in a rain of biomass. The legacy of the Nameless Ones remakes him, casts him to his final purpose. Bids him rise to his—feet?—and into the unsealed airlock. He clutches at one of the heavy EVA suits, hanging in its cradle.

Do I even need this? he wonders with a start. His faith is not quite assured though, so Pike prepares the vacuum suit.

The deck vibrates beneath his feet. The comet, black and luminous, now sets against the horizon of the airlock's crystal porthole. *No!*

The crew are firing the thrusters, and *Grass is Greener* turgidly aims away from its most desired fate.

Fight it, he implores the ship, but their connection has been severed. It remains at the mercy of its infidel crew. A sudden crash throws him back. An anguished shudder groans through the bulkheads. His ears pop as pressure equalizes.

The EVA suit's umbilical is still plugged into its charging port. Awakened biomass drips into the life support pack, black and green ooze. With shaking hands, Pike loosens the EVA suit from its main harness. The weight of it nearly drags him to the deck, but he's stronger. He expects new flares of agony, but the pain remains distant like a storm cloud on a drought-bright horizon.

Emergency strobes jab red daggers into his eyes. Rainbows of color dance at the edges of his vision. *Tick-tick-click-braae—eeeee!* The comm's signal skates down his optic nerve, burrowing into his brain like a sod worm in a wet field. Bringing understanding. Bringing calm.

Swaying, he stumbles into the baggy legs of the EVA suit. Its haptic cilia, woven from simple strands of biotic muscles, hug his calves, his thighs. Welcoming him inside.

What remains of his arms, fraying into a million cilia themselves, wind through the sleeves of the EVA suit and into the locking gauntlets. With the joining of cilia—biotic with fleshy—Pike moves the fingers of the suit as easily as if they were his own. He laughs, reveling in the warmth that spreads through him.

He hasn't felt this full of light in seventy-five years.

"Open up, you bastard." The grating contralto of the captain interrupts his ecstasy.

The synthetic appears at the airlock door port. She's splattered with the ship's awakened biomass. Pike dares to hope she's been chosen by the ship too, but the vexation pinching her face says otherwise. She taps the window with the slim barrel of a UGM-75 needler.

A good weapon but no longer any threat to him.

"Captain," Pike grimaces a hello through another wave of dizziness. Civility will distract her. For all their intellect, synthetics are terrible at subterfuge.

"Tell me what you did to my ship."

The synthetic talks tough, but he still sees the fear in her eyes. She's wondering if the change will affect her biotic components too. Perhaps it can, but Pike's plans won't wait for an uncertain ally, even a synthetic one.

"Guess a man can't ever travel too far from what he was born to, Captain. I'm a farmer to the bone." He giggles, wondering what happened to the bones in his arms.

The synthetic isn't amused by his confession. She glares supernovas as the needler drops out of sight. One of her hands works at the door controls.

"I planted a seed, a *spore*, Captain," he explains, hoping to keep the distraction going. "*Grass is Greener* has joined the pilgrimage to the realm of the Nameless Ones. We are all welcome to join it."

She hesitates. Her shining yellow eyes regard him in confusion. He doesn't expect a sliver of understanding from a synthetic on metaphysical matters, but her ignorance still angers him. Ghosts of agony flit through his chest, reminding him he has little time to educate the unfaithful. Yet Brother Hong never turned down an opportunity to share an evangelical lesson.

"The Nameless Ones, Captain. They oozed through the primordial dark at the beginning of all things. All life arose out of the residue of their couplings. We are their imperfect progeny."

The synthetic looks confused, so Pike skips the rest of the sermon.

"Biotic technology was developed by studying the lost science of the Nameless Ones. We shunt in and out of warp according to *their* designs."

"The biomass has infected your brain, Pike." She continues to work on the door.

"Maybe," he admits. "But what of your own synthetic brain? Have you considered you're not immune to the call of the Nameless Ones? You're the navigator after all. You brought us straight to the comet."

His words strike the synthetic deep. She freezes, an all-to-human shock playing across her all-too-perfect face.

Pike releases the suit's helmet from the charger and detaches the biomass umbilical from the top.

The captain raises her useless needler.

"Fuck your dead gods. You killed three members of my crew, Pike."

He mimics her pained expression. "Revenge? Please. We're way past that. This is history, Captain. Destiny."

"Destiny?" the synthetic shrieks, reddening with anger. Pike shrugs and places the helmet over his head. He doesn't have time to convert her, he can't make her see. Perhaps *Grass is Greener* can when they reach the comet's orbit. The synthetic continues to shout, but her words are lost in the hiss of pressure as his helmet seals.

"Goodbye, Captain. Perhaps we'll see each other again in the gaze of the Nameless Ones."

The synthetic screams again, her face nearly split open with her anger. Pike smiles, pitying her woeful lack of understanding.

The status lights inside his helmet's heads-up display turn green. The fuel and oxygen meters on his suit read full. *It's time to see if you've borne fruit, Brother Hong.* A crawling agony ripples through his chest. He feels a loosening as if his ribs have dissolved. His throat is wet, swollen. So be it. Pain is its own excitement, the only marker of his passage into history.

Pike elects not to activate his suit's comm. Nothing the captain says will stop him. He knows what he needs to do. She mouths, "Don't you dare," as he twists the final seal on the helmet. Her image fades as the helmet polarizes, and the blood rushes from Pike's head.

"See you soon, Mama," he whispers and opens the outer door of the airlock.

Pike drifts into space, into destiny.

Lira runs back through the infirmary toward the central crew lifts. Pike has blasted himself into space, but she has a curious feeling that he's still a threat to the ship and everyone aboard. He was so sure of himself, so smug.

Are his gods imagined? Lira worries that perhaps they aren't or that, more accurately, some flaw in the centuries-old biotic technology has a vulnerability to impulses from warp space (if not puppet-strings to malevolent space deities).

Her synthetic biology may have been developed from the same tech as *Grass is Greener*, but she's several orders of magnitude more complex: a human to a nematode. If the biotic cores of ships are susceptible to those impulses, what did that say about the brains of the synthetics who interfaced with them?

Such speculation is ridiculous.

Near the lifts, she finds a locker with four light-duty EVA suits hanging like deflated deckhands. Their biotic umbilicals, attached to an auxiliary cradle, still shine with blue-green luminescence.

Lira sighs with relief, strips out of her coveralls, and shrugs into a suit. The haptic cilia wriggle to life, snugging the fit and kicking off the oxygen exchange. The comm unit on the wall emits a constant squawk of static now. Like a hellbent rider, the post-stim headache charges in on the back of the grating noise. Lira rubs her temples.

If interfacing with the biotic core of *Grass is Greener* is what caused this nightmare, then perhaps it would also get them out of it. It also increased the probability that Pike jettisoned himself out the airlock not to escape but to re-enter the ship somewhere else—like the airlock doors they'd just opened on the engineering deck.

She presses the button for the bridge, and there's a variation of the squeal that might be Abe or Driscoll replying. It drones in her eardrums, worsening the headache.

"Abe. Driscoll. Anyone who can hear me," she croaks. "Get suited up immediately. Environment is contaminated. Meet me in engineering. I think Pike is headed there."

It's where she would go if she wanted to try a last-ditch effort to steer *Grass is Greener* away from—or into—the comet. The heart of the vessel, and they'd left the door open. Pike's suit had an EVA thruster. He is probably flying right back inside.

There's an answering burst of noise on the comm. She hopes that her crew heard her commands. Waiting even seconds for them to respond would waste time they didn't have.

Her heart hammering, Lira opens the lift. She finds her stunner rifle on the threshold, coated in biomass but still showing a full charge. It might not be much good against Pike in his hardened EVA suit, but it's better than the damn needler.

Her suit's internal comms crackle once.

"Lira . . . read me?"

Abe. Thank god.

"Where are you?" she demands.

"You weren't responding on the ship comms," Abe says. "Figured I'd try the suit frequencies."

"Pike could be listening," she warns. "He went out the airlock in a suit."

"Acknowledged. Switching to emergency channel." After a pause, Abe continues. "On my way down to engineering via the ladderwells."

"The others?"

"Right here, Captain!" answers Driscoll. "My ass is still on the bridge." Despite his sarcasm, he sounds relieved to hear from her. "You get that saint of dicks?" he asks eagerly.

"Negative. I believe he's headed for the B-Deck airlock."

"I'll fire the thrusters again," Driscoll suggests. "That ought to throw him off course a bit. I only got three minutes of burn left though."

"Do it. Even if he gets back aboard, we need all the distance we can get from the comet."

"Sure, Lira. And then?"

"Set the autopilot. Nasr, you listening?"

"Yeah."

There's shouting in the background, and a scream.

"What's going on down there, Fidda?'

"Not all the passengers want to go to the lifepods, Captain. There's a group blocking the way."

Saints of shit.

"Stun the ones who won't go. Drag them into the pods if you must."

"Sir?" Nasr says.

"*Grass is Greener* is lost, Nasr. The biotics are infected with some sort of virus. We can't save the ship, but dammit, we must try and save the lives aboard it."

"Yes, Captain," Nasr says, sounding lost.

"Driscoll, you fire those thrusters and go help Nasr. She needs you."

"Aye," he says.

Nasr moans in her suit comm, and Lira hopes Driscoll gets down there quickly.

"Callum's with me," interjects Abe. "Should I send her up to help them?"

"No," Lira says. "I want three of us waiting for Pike if he gets back in."

"We'll get him," a confident Callum assures her.

The lift shudders to a stop, but the airlock needs to cycle before it lets her pass into the decompressed deck. Thirty more seconds. Lira checks the seals on her helmet.

"Be careful. He's got something planned in engineering. I believe he thinks he can communicate directly with the core."

That elicits an amused bark from Abe.

"Not even you can do that, Lira. Hells, I've been tending *Grass is Greener* for decades, and it's beyond me too."

"I'm concerned that he can. Through the infection somehow. He seems to have the idea he's on some sort of religious crusade. A fanatic is dangerous, Abe."

"*Grass is Greener* isn't going anywhere, no matter how nicely he asks." Abe's wry amusement just barely hides the defeat in his tone. No matter how nicely Abe asks either.

Several moments of silence tick by as the air drains from the airlock. Abe bursts back onto the suit comms.

"I'm back in engineering. It's bad, Lira. The door's jammed tight, and the decompression just spread the mess around inside like you feared. Worse, the airlock doors aren't responding."

Lira sighs as the lift finally shudders open and admits her to the airless ruin of B-Deck. Abe wasn't exaggerating. The walls are caked with black scabs of flash-frozen biomass. It hangs like burnt skin from bulkheads. The deck beneath her trembles, the vibrations magnified by the cilia in her suit. A weak but steady hum reaches her ears.

"Someone's fired up the main drive!" Abe shouts in the comm.

"It's Pike!" Callum warns. "He's inside the compartment!"

The bitter ache of failure closes Lira's throat.

"Nasr, Driscoll, abandon ship. Get our passengers to the lifepods no matter how."

Over their comms, Lira hears the *blatt-blatt* of stunner fire. Nasr gives an inarticulate shout. Her comms fill with the heavy sound of the deckhand's breathing.

The bulkheads thrum with a secondary vibrato—Driscoll firing the thrusters.

"Done! What about the rest of you?" the quartermaster asks.

"We're going to stop Pike first," Abe answers. Three hollow, rhythmic bangs ring out from Abe's end.

"Abe? Callum?"

Ice water freezes her veins. Lira's chest squeezes so tight she's afraid her synthetic heart will fail. She races toward engineering as fast as her suit will allow. She's got to save them. No. She *will* save them. Hatches bang closed around her, triggered by Pike or the reflexes of her dying vessel, Lira doesn't know. She slides under the main hatch to B-Deck just as it clangs shut.

With an eyeblink, she switches the comms back to a public channel. "Are you listening, Pike?" she asks, but the question might as well be directed to *Grass is Greener*. "There are no Nameless Ones. No alien gods waiting in a warp-space paradise. No one else is going to die today for your demented crusade. You hear me?"

A triple squawk of static is the only reply.

The EVA flight is a short one. As soon as he's blasted from the airlock, Pike fires the suit's thruster pack, arcing him around *Grass is Greener,* cleaving to the bosom of the knobby hull. He streaks past the observation viewports where vacant-eyed passengers stare.

Sensor vanes and other biotic spars thrust from the hull, threatening to impale him. But the Nameless Ones guide his hand past razor-sharp solar arrays and eminences of radioactive thruster exhaust to the yawning airlock just aft of engineering. The opening is dark as a pit and festooned with the writhing shadows of flash-frozen biomass.

Pike plunges through, his sense of elation and urgency waxing to a feverish pitch. He's done it! After a short thrust down a cold and lightless corridor, he's at the main hatch of engineering itself. He seals himself inside just as a blaze of helmet lights appear down the opposite corridor. More crew, no doubt, intent on terminating his holy mission, but they will fail.

They're already too late.

The engineering compartment is much as he left it: a ruin of shattered metal and biotic components. But the spore has encouraged a new and fecund growth. Bulbous cylinders of glistening, charcoal flesh sprout from the bulkheads, branching into waving stalks like the anemones of Oleander. Gossamer curtains of biomass drape across every surface, clinging to the drive cowlings like funereal crepe.

It's no death he's witnessing, Pike knows. It's a birth. And not just for the ship.

He feels the nativity deep within his own boneless flesh as a pulsing gray light, a soon-to-be dazzling eruption of fire and joy. Biomass stalks jut from his suit's shoulders, moss-covered spines that quiver like antennae in the airless compartment. His own shoulders ache with the weight of them. Have they merely grown from the suit, or are they rooted in his very self? Pike cannot tell.

Not that Pike has much time for contemplating his newfound constitution.

Grass is Greener calls urgently to him, an insistent keening. He kneels in the engine well next to the main drive cowlings. The corpse of the engineer has fused to the deck, his mouth gaping in a mummified scream. He has not been reborn, alas, but Pike utters a prayer to the Nameless Ones that they might find use for his lost soul all the same.

A sharp pain focuses what remains of his mind. The ship needs him if they are to reach the comet. *Grass is Greener* shows him why. The comet is gathering spacetime around it, folding the leaves of existence into a vast cocoon. When the folding is done, when the last threads of its spacetime chrysalis have been spun, the mysterious comet will depart Pike's current understanding of existence.

He feels the tickle of Brother Hong's breath on his neck. Pike is so close now. The Nameless Ones have called him to join their eternal voyage. He must not fail to answer.

Pike drops to all fours near one of the drive shrouds. The deck is freeze-dried, half-melted from the unchecked biotic cancer. He digs the bulky fingers of his gloves into the soft metal. Fistfuls of biomass and deck plating yield to his tearing. Sparks fly, stinging his suit-flesh. Power junctions smoke and flame. At the ferry's prodding, Pike digs his way deeper, past the mundane mechanical and electrical systems, plunging into coils of glistening biotic veins and pulsing lymph nodes. A fetid odor rises in his helmet. Pike breathes the scent deeply, remembering the fertilized rows of wheat-sedge and the bright, hot winds of Crockett. His heart thunders, matching the palpitations of the biotic heart of *Grass is Greener*, quaking far below.

He stands waist deep in a grotto half-machine and half-flesh and wonders, *What will the ship ask of him when he reaches that great and monolithic heart?*

Pike is no expert on ship propulsion systems, but he dimly recalls that the biotic organs that make warp-shifting possible are sealed within vast and impenetrable housings. They are never meant to be accessed directly during the operation of a ship. If he continues burrowing toward the delirious gravity of the core, then what happens to him? Will the suit protect him? Will his flesh finish dissolving into the gray and terrible light of the Nameless Ones?

The pressure of the ferry's hunger squeezes against his momentary shell of resistance. Cracks appear. A vital warmth floods his limbs, drawing him down. Drawing him toward an enfolding slumber.

No, Mama, he thinks. *I'm not ready for bed.*

Pike swallows.

Boom.

Boom.

Boom.

There's a pounding in his soul—but also at the hatch to engineering. Shadows and stars move beyond the viewport, the shout of amplified and angry voices. The throaty whine of a plasma drill joins the chorus, jerking Pike away from his apotheosis and back to a fleshy and imperfect awareness. The ignorant crew has set upon him once again, but it only steels his resolve to complete his last mortal task.

Durance Pike raises his hands to his face. The gloves are now unrecognizable, crusted with thorny growths and cruel, sharp talons. The corners of his mouth curve up in a beatific but lightless smile as he turns to greet the unbelievers.

Abe and Callum are at the engineering hatch in light-duty EVA suits, backlit by the brilliant ruby flare of Abe's plasma drill. Lira joins them, her visor automatically darkening against the almost solar glare. Stim-withdrawal carves a headache in three deep ridges around her skull. The inside of her helmet smells of ammonia. Her eyes sting.

Has she been infected?

With both hands, Abe guides his cutting beam neatly around the hatch's locking mechanism. Callum readies her stunner, assuming a soldier's stance. Lira reaches over and flips the dial on her rifle to full power, and Callum gives a stiff nod of thanks. Lira does the same with her own gun, hoping a sustained assault will be enough to stop Pike, even in his EVA suit.

Nasr's channel fuzzes with static and the occasional blast of a stunner. She's stopped answering Lira's calls.

She doesn't have time to worry. The drill beam cuts off, plunging the passageway back into semi-twilight. Their suit lights scrape the bulkheads, illuminating the festering biotic tumors that ring the hatch.

"Ready, Lira?" Abe says. His jocular manner has vanished with the drill beam. He sounds as lost as his beloved *Grass is Greener*.

Lira attempts to steady him with a hand on his pauldron. Her hand shakes violently. Perhaps it still helps. Abe nods, his face grave.

He kicks the scored door in, firing up the drill once more. Abe and Callum rush into the compartment. Her stunner blasts strobe like emergency lights in the narrow space. Lira races in behind them, casting her own stun bolts at the hulking shadow that rises from the floor.

The specter moves fast, scything out with an elongated arm at Callum. The deckhand screams, and her comm goes silent as she bounces against the oddly flexing deck. Her stunner, still firing, skips once and disappears into a huge trench carved between the engine cowlings.

Abe turns the star-flare burn of the drill on the monster that Pike has become. The hellish light strips away the shadows, revealing the bulky EVA suit Pike had donned on the upper decks. It's barely recognizable, slathered with knobby growths of biomass and ridged with wavering spines on the shoulders and back like some perverse deep-sea fish. Pike's face is no longer visible either, his visor instead emitting a green and putrid glow.

With another swipe of his monstrous arms, Pike knocks the drill, still burning, from Abe's hands. The laser flare slices neatly through the engineer's left arm as it crashes heavily to the deck. Abe's screams fill her ears.

Lira squeezes the trigger of her stunner on full charge, snarling as each bolt sizzles against Pike's suit. The bolts don't slow him down at all. He lurches across the deck and backhands Lira across the faceplate. An oxygen warning chime sounds, followed by a loud hissing, leaving her short of breath. Lira collapses against a railing, landing on her side. The helmet patches itself with a gooey polymer that keeps the air leak from worsening.

Callum rolls on the spongy deck, clutching at a spike of thorny biomass jutting from her stomach. Her screaming is silent. Gravity is failing, and glittering red jewels float from her wound into the tomb-like stillness of the compartment. Abe, his good arm dangling, slumps to his knees. His ragged panting fogs up his visor until Lira cannot see his anguished face. Unlike Callum, his voice comm is still switched on.

"Sisterfucker, sisterfucker," he moans, his voice raw.

Lira, still senseless from Pike's superhuman blow, gazes past the frost forming around the cracks in her visor to see the madman—no, the mad *thing*—resuming its crazed digging into the engine deck. The top of its spike-barnacled helmet dips in and out of view, throwing back the dull, greenish reflection of her suit lights.

Her stunner lies just past her trembling fingertips, but she doesn't bother to reach for it. It won't do any good anyway.

Abe's suit has sealed around the torn ruin of his left arm, but shock has deepened his slump. Callum's motionless, save for a small twitch of her right boot. Her foot almost seems detached, too much like Magnus Lin's, sticking out from that first terrible burst of infected biomass.

Lira doesn't want to cease functioning here, another boot poking out from the tumorous undergrowth of a dead biotic vessel. That outcome finally stirs her to action. She pushes herself up, weaving in the dying gravity and the uncertain footing of the elastic surface. She'll never save the ship, but she can try and save something. Abe, moaning softly, is light in her arms as she lifts him to his feet.

She drags him from engineering with only a glance back to the hole Pike is digging. She can no longer see the bouncing helmet. Pike has descended to depths unknown, and as far as Lira's concerned, he can dig himself to hell.

It's a long crawl up the ladderwells to the starboard lifepods. Most have been launched, but a distant moaning from behind the hatches of A-Deck makes Lira question how many passengers they contained when they launched. From Nasr, there's no word, and Driscoll fails to answer her frantic calls over the comm. At least the comet has, for now, slipped to the port of the ship, and her launch path is free from its baleful gaze.

As she activates the emergency flight systems, the comms fill with the incessant whine of the ferry, a plaintive call to stay with the ship.

Maybe Pike's right, comes the unsettling thought. *Perhaps Grass is Greener led me here as much as it did him.*

If the Nameless Ones still call to Lira when the pod launches, she cannot hear them in the roar of the thrusters. *Let her feet be planet-bound after today.* She and Abe will bury themselves on some agriworld, like seeds taking root. They'll live out their days far from biotic minds and hearts as long as there are plenty of stims at hand.

The secondary boosters fire, hurling the pod far from the comet and into deep space. As it presses Lira against the acceleration couch, she looks over at Abe, relieved to hear his faint, bemused laughter over the comm.

As he slips into a fevered sleep, her relief turns to horror when she notices the black fuzz of biomass growing just inside his helmet.

A hot wind blows across the sandy earth. Rance Pike studies the barren crop rows that stretch beyond him from bright horizon to bright horizon. He's only eight, yet he towers over the stunted and ruined crop. Somewhere near the end of one field, their domed hovel squats in a narrow defile, shielded from the worst of the summer winds but not the dry rot that has destroyed their farm and doomed Mama.

Rance carries a little shovel, the kind you'd use in a backyard garden, and a handful of unfamiliar, hard black seeds he knows Mama's never planted before. Clipped to his belt is a little canteen of water from the air condenser under the house. It sloshes, almost empty.

"Rance!"

Mama's voice calls, thin and weak, from the depths of the house. Even the howling winds of Crockett can't summon a tenth of the despair he hears in Mama's call.

He takes a step toward the farmhouse and stops. He looks at the seeds and at the shovel—at the endless acres of lifeless dirt that surrounds him. He'd promised his brother that he'd plant the seeds and thought that he had. Yet here he stands out in the field still clutching the tiny spores in his small brown hand.

Mama's sick, but he's only eight. Surely, she can't expect him to tend to all these fields with so little. Not even both of them, working sunup to sundown, have been able to save the farm. How could he do it alone?

"Raaaance!"

Mama breaks off, wracked by another spasm of coughing. He should go to her, comfort her in her final hour. But the field needs planting. How else will he eat when she's gone?

Another sound haunts the air above the winds. Engines. The whine of an approaching AGC scout, looking to foreclose on another ruined property.

Rance doesn't know what to do. The AGC man will offer him a lot of money to walk away, and he'll use big words that will make Rance's head hurt. He could go in with Mama and wait it out. In any case, he probably ought to at least plant the seeds first.

Maybe that would make AGC and Mama both happy.

Maybe it would even bring the farm back.

"Rance!"

In the distance, a blunt-nosed shuttle lands, raising dust devils and storms of papery wheat-sedge husks.

He starts for the farmhouse even as the corporate agent calls to him. In the life before, he went to the AGC agent first, and his pockets were bulging with credits by the end of the week. His canteen was full forever after that. But Mama still died, and he never got to tell her goodbye.

This time, he would.

PART 2: CONVEX DISSIPATION OF STARLIGHT

The tropical sun is warm on Lira's skin and falls in dappled rays through the broad-leafed trees that crowd the jungle path to Abe's memorial. Summer hasn't yet come to the island, and the air buzzes with memories.

Lira sighs, stung by some of those memories. It was a day like this when they arrived on Abe's tropical home world of Oleander, wounded and reeling from the ordeal on *Grass is Greener*: Abe's body had been irretrievably wrecked, his mind clouded and failing. They walked these wild trails near their home for nearly ten years before he died. Lira walks them still.

Far below the hidden cliffs to her left, the ocean roars an unceasing song. The drone of insects and the calls of birds add to the symphony. It's a fitting tribute to Abe's memory. He'd died five years ago this morning, after being in a coma for nearly a year. She didn't even get to say a proper goodbye. Later, she spread his ashes over his beloved sea.

Still drifting on the bittersweet tides of memory, Lira rounds the path into the remote clearing—a pilgrimage she's made every year since. She freezes with surprise as a woman, a stranger, rises from Abe's concrete marker.

A fresh bouquet of cheap purple flowers—no doubt picked up at the village a three-kilometer hike east—lies at the base of the marker.

The woman has clay-dark skin, typical of most Oleander islanders, but she's no visiting neighbor. Her black hair's shorn close like a spacer's, and she wears a crisp jumpsuit that looks vaguely military. She doesn't seem armed, but Lira adopts a guarded stance, wishing she had her needler. The one she clutches tight in the dark after waking from nightmares of tilting starships overgrown with biotic fungus.

"Who are you?" Lira demands. She tenses for a fight.

"You're Lira." The woman smiles, clearly trying to put Lira at ease, but a trace of anxiety in her amber eyes suggests duplicity behind a mask of geniality. Something sad too. Lira frowns, remembering the flowers the woman placed at the memorial. She'd known Abe somehow, but Lira can't recall meeting her before.

"Who are you?" Lira repeats, a little kindlier.

The woman offers her hand—Oleander style, palm up—but Lira keeps her distance at the edge of the clearing. Her gesture rebuffed, the woman nods, her smile tightening. "I'm Captain Nikela Abreu of the packet tramp *Convex Dissipation of Starlight*."

Lira doesn't recognize the name, and Abreu seems too young to have been a crewmate from her Mosquito Fleet days. Still, from the lead weight settling in her gut, she can't shake the feeling that her past is catching up with her.

"Why are you here?" she asks Abreu.

"I desperately need a navigator, Lira, and"—she glances back at Abe's memorial—"I hope you'll sign on to my crew."

The lead weight in Lira cracks, and a tingling sensation spreads up her spine to the base of her neck. "I'm retired."

Abreu's smile grows again. She'd clearly anticipated that answer. "Right. I'm hoping to change your mind. But I shouldn't discuss it out here. Do you have someplace private we can talk?"

To her great surprise, Lira finds herself nodding agreement, though she's more interested in Abreu's connection to Abe than in any desire to ever leave Oleander again.

After all, she'd promised Abe she wouldn't.

Nikela Abreu suppresses a frown as the synthetic pours boiling water from an electric kettle into two plain clay cups. A sharp citrus smell fills the kitchen. Lemon, or something similar, and the fungal undertones of biotic tea in the steam. Maintenance for Lira's synthetic cells and the secret to why she appears twenty years younger than her actual seventy operational years. The tea's safe enough for Nikela to drink even if she knows she won't like the flavor. She gratefully accepts the cup, though she could have lived her whole life without coming face to face with this particular synthetic human.

Saints of shit, she hadn't been ready to see that memorial in the jungle either.

You don't have many choices, love, she tells herself. AgriGrow—the Company—needs *this* navigator. And *she* needs Lira too.

Nikela sips the acerbic tea, trying not to let her worries show. She studies the modest kitchen to distract herself from the taste. The living space is a prefab structure—not as primitive as she'd assumed after reading Lira's file, but spare. Plain walls, functional cooker. Devoid of sentimental clutter. Like a spacer's quarters. Nikela approves of *that* at least.

"Alright, Captain Abreu," Lira says, leaning against the countertop opposite her, "no more stalling. Why are you here?"

Nikela sets the cup aside, wishing Lira would just sit down. "As I said before, I want to hire a navigator."

A brittle irritation flashes in Lira's crystalline eyes. "There are dozens of freelance navigators, synthetic and otherwise, who'd be delighted to take a new contract. Yet you come to one of the remotest districts on Oleander, looking for me. You must know my service record. So why me?"

Nikela scowls. Fine, she can do blunt if the navigator prefers it. "Crockett," Nikela says, almost relishing the look of horror that crosses Lira's face. "We're going to Crockett."

"Virgin's taint you are. That system's under interdict by the Colonial Navy. You'll be fried to atoms if you get anywhere within—

Lira narrows her eyes. "Unless *you're* Colonial Navy."

Nikela maintains a neutral expression. Lira's wrong, but it's better to let her believe that for now. If she knew who was really funding this expedition, she'd never agree to go.

"Officially, we're an independent mail packet," Nikela allows, "and we don't have the authorization to break the interdict. But we're going, and no one knows that system like you, Lira."

That much is all true.

Crockett was once an agriworld, one of the most fertile in the Spin Colonies. Nikela moved there with her mom after her dad took off. Fields of endless grain, waving green and gold—wheat-sedge and a dozen other crops—enough to feed the colonies. Then came the Blight. AgriGrow Corporation tried to fix things, and they made progress, but then that rogue comet fell, poisoning the world forever.

Lira had been one of the first to see the strange comet. She'd seen what it could do firsthand.

That's why Nikela wants her. And Lira knows it.

Lira doesn't answer, pouring more tea instead.

Nikela tries another tack. "What happened on *Grass is Greener*—"

The synthetic explodes with anger. "We barely survived that fucking disaster. My partner and I came to Oleander so that we'd never go through anything like it again."

"Your partner," Nikela says, the words like ashes in her mouth. If only Lira knew the truth about Abraham Mistri.

Lira, noting her tone, turns wary again. "What does this have to do with Abe?"

Nikela flushes, angry at herself for reacting. She'd hoped to hook Lira with intrigue alone, but it's clear that she'd been naive. Mistri she'll save for later. She has bigger bait to dangle.

"What do you know of the man called Durance Pike?"

Lira's expression is stony. "That he's sisterfucking dead," she spits, her final word on the subject.

Now who's being naive? Nikela digs out the holocube from the pouch at her belt. The metal clicks as she sets it on the table.

"May I?"

The synthetic nods, tight-lipped, and Nikela toggles the activator.

A ghostly image fuzzes to life above Lira's kitchen table. Shot by the Company's autonomous survey unit, it shows indistinct heavy machinery, agricultural equipment at an old wheat sedge storage complex. Nikela's studied the footage countless times. She almost pities Lira, knowing what she's about to see. It wasn't easy for *her* the first time either.

The image shifts, focusing on mounds of grain slick with rot. Gossamer curtains of biotic growth dangle from above. One of the mounds shudders, rises, plunging the ASU into deep shadow. There's a frantic scramble of colors as the probe switches to other bands, attempting to penetrate the sudden darkness.

Nikela peers through the grainy holo. Lira's eyes are flat, her expression unreadable. The corner of her mouth twitches as the probe documents braided ropes of biotic growth studded with bell-shaped fruiting bodies, each the size of a fist. The ropey tendrils slither around a ringed aperture of teeth, parting to reveal a half-fleshed human head. Bone gleams in the probe's light as the head turns to face it.

The skull wears the grinning face of Durance Pike.

Lira grunts and clutches the table until her knuckles turn white. Holo-Pike stares with bloodshot, newborn eyes.

"Help me," the holo says.

Pike grimaces and vanishes once more into the ropey mass. Moments later, the probe's feed goes dead.

The teacup rattles in Lira's pale, shaking hands.

"This is fabricated," she accuses Nikela, her eyes glittering with sudden tears. "I watched him crawl into the heart of a biotic stardrive. No one survives that."

"I wish it were," Nikela says, edging away from the woman's obvious distress. She truly does understand. "The comm-stamp is current and verified, Lira. This message was sent less than three months ago."

"Verified?" Lira slams the teacup into the sink, shattering the clay cup. "By *whom*?"

"I'm not at liberty to say," Nikela explains, "but—"

"You're no packet ship captain, Abreu. And I will not set foot on a military vessel."

Nikela raises a placating hand.

"We're *not* military," she assures her, "and we can pay you very well."

"I don't want your shitting money," Lira says.

Nikela sighs. She could just summon her crew and have Lira dragged aboard, but that's her last resort. So she gambles, deciding to tell Lira a little more than the NDAs technically permitted.

"We believe Pike allowed himself to be recorded. He *wants* us to find him."

"Then that's the last fucking thing you should do," Lira replies.

"Nonetheless, I'm going, and I'd like to have your help. You know him. This might be our chance to understand what's happening on Crockett. What happened on *Grass is Greener*. What happened to Abe."

Lira scowls. "I know what happened, Captain," she says quietly. "He died in this house five years ago."

"Did he?" Nikela says.

She narrows her eyes, her expression cold. "What did you just say?"

Nikela takes a deep breath. Remorse makes the back of her throat ache. Fine, she'll play this move. She would have preferred to save it for leverage later. "Lira, there are answers on Crockett. About Pike, yes, but Abraham Mistri too. I want to know exactly what happened to him on *Grass is Greener*. I deserve to know. He's my father."

Lira recoils. She stares, slack-jawed, even paler than before. Nikela scores herself a point and allows a small triumphant grin to spread across her face. She can see it in Lira's sapphire eyes.

She's got her navigator.

2.

How I've missed you.

Lira dozes in bed, entwined with Abe and his sleepy declarations, warm and solid and real next to her.

Why didn't you tell me about your daughter? Lira says.

With her question, a sharp ammonia reek sears Lira's nose, burns her eyes. Abe shifts, his skin wrinkled and fuzzing over with green-black mold. Lira can't breathe. She struggles to free herself from his tangled, fungal limbs. Their bedroom tumbles violently, tossed on the invisible currents of spacetime that stream from the sinister comet. Black vines grow across the walls, dangling curtains of yellow slime.

It's just a dream, Lira, Abe's voice coos, *but I still miss you . . .*

The ship's bell chimes four times, jolting Lira fully awake. She fumbles with the hypersleep cuff.

"Abe?" she croaks, knowing he won't answer. He never does. The images of their corrupted bedroom fade.

She starts from her bunk and stares at the chrono, listening. The cabin Abreu assigned her is not much larger than her bunk. A suspiciously sleek mail-packet vessel, bristling with military-grade comms and sensor vanes. If not Colonial Navy, then who?

No insignia anywhere, not aboard ship nor on the plain gray jumpsuits of the crew. Not even a faked company logo.

Lira's been aboard twelve hours, and they haven't allowed her a proper interface to talk to the ship yet. She has no sense of the biotic systems, but its emissions seem dampened somehow. Shielded. She hasn't seen so much as a single exposed hydraulic conduit since she came on board. *Just who in the hell are these people?*

Lira admits to herself that maybe she doesn't care. She has another shot at Pike. That's all that matters.

Pike or some iteration of him, a virulent cancer repurposed by biotic rot.

Even more, she wants to know what Nikela Abreu can tell her about Abe, Nikela's father. She hinted he might still be alive. Is Lira lonely enough to harbor some foolish hope she's right? Abreu had avoided all further discussion since they came aboard, focusing instead on jump coordinates and possible approaches to Pike. *She's hiding something though,* Lira thinks.

It unsettles Lira so much that her hands shake. She quit the stimbulbs long ago, but the pains of the old habit spark through her nerves like a sticky circuit.

The bulkheads start to tremble with deceleration in seeming sympathy with her own inner turmoil. It's a long burn downsystem, especially since they are dropping out of warp space so far outside the standard routes. Captain Abreu said they'd be slipping through the navy's sensor fields at a blind spot. Not that Lira can verify that. Abreu had confined her to quarters until the microjump closer to orbit. That's when they'd need Lira's biotic expertise.

The strange tangle of quantum gradients surrounding Crockett is even worse than what streamed off the comet all those years ago. Abreu has tasked Lira with plotting a course through them, a microjump through the fluctuating quantum shear. Good thing *Convex* is fast; the gradients would have torn the lumbering *Grass is Greener* to shreds no matter what path Lira found through the spacetime maze.

She glances at her datatab and last night's equations. She's done the best she could without a communion with *Convex*.

As if reading her thoughts, the comm chimes again with an expectant beep.

She toggles the channel open. *Time to report for duty.* "Lira," she answers.

"Good morning, Navigator," comes Abreu's brisk, cheerful reply. "We'll need you on the bridge in fifteen minutes."

"Right," she says, "on my way."

Whatever Abreu's got planned on Crockett, Lira will have some answers soon—assuming she doesn't scatter their atoms in the microjump.

Concerned, Nikela releases the comm switch and lingers outside the hatch to cargo bay one. Lira hadn't sounded too eager about reporting to the bridge. Maybe it should worry her. After all, as she'd said, the navigator had a terrible service record. *Highline* and *Grass is Greener* are the worst marks on her record, but they aren't the only ones. The Company's actuaries also calculated there's a small chance Lira might sabotage the mission out of some grudge against what happened over Crockett fifteen years ago.

Nikela doubts that. Pike killed a lot of Lira's people on *Grass is Greener*. She might want revenge, but nothing in her record suggested she'd risk her crew—Nikela's crew—to get it.

Then there's the matter of their shared history with that bastard Abraham Mistri. Nikela's dad. She knows things about him that Lira doesn't—like there were other anomalous signals the Company received from Crockett. The navigator won't forfeit a chance for a reunion. Nikela winces to herself, admitting the Company might be using the same tactics on her.

She opens the hatch to the cargo bay. Mai waits at attention inside. The lieutenant is a synthetic like Lira. Unlike the navigator though, the bounds of her loyalty are thoroughly mapped.

"Sir!" she shouts as Nikela comes through the hatch.

"At ease, Lieutenant," Nikela commands, lowering her voice as if Lira might hear her two decks down. "We're meant to be a packet ship."

"I doubt the navigator buys the ruse," Mai replies, resuming a squat-postured seat on a cargo crate that's supposed to be packed with holo mail and supplies. It actually contains forty-eight armor piercing grenades. *And those aren't even the biggest booms onboard,* Nikela muses with a twinge of guilt.

She studies Lieutenant Mai, hoping to the saints she won't need to activate Failsafe Protocols.

"Deniability, Lieutenant," Nikela explains. "Not even the Navy knows we're here."

Mai nods, accepting that, but the question lingers in her eyes. She wants to know what they'll find down on Crockett.

Nikela paces the cargo bay. She trusts Mai more than anyone else on the ship, but the Company's NDAs are strict, even with regard to other essential operational personnel.

"It's a recon mission, Mai. And a possible retrieval."

Mai nods. "What sort of retrieval, sir? We've trained for at least a dozen different scenarios, and it would help—"

"We'll see," Nikela interrupts.

Mai turns thoughtful, but she doesn't press. Nikela hasn't known the synthetic long, but she's loyal.

"Do you think we can trust Lira?" Mai asks instead.

"I think she wants to see what's down there as much as we do, Lieutenant."

And it's the truth. Nikela's desperate to peer below that churn of spacetime surrounding Crockett. Beyond the Company's directives, she wants answers about Mistri and Pike too.

Mai taps the side of her shaved head. She's a soldier. She's designed to imagine the worst outcomes. "I mean in *here*, sir. I read the reports about *Grass is Greener*. Biotic contagion affected more than just the ship."

Older model synthetics were, at least in theory, more susceptible to biotic contagion, but Nikela isn't worried.

"It's been fifteen years since *Grass is Greener*," Nikela assures her. "I think we'd know by now if she'd been infected. But all the same, if Lira starts behaving oddly, you do have your orders, Lieutenant."

"Of course, sir. No problems there."

Mai seems to want to say more, her fingers reflexively tapping her hips where her sidearm usually rested.

"What if it's *me* that starts acting oddly, sir?" Mai asks.

Nikela can't meet the synthetic's questioning violet eyes. The Company's Failsafe Protocols would handle that.

"I've got no worries about you, Lieutenant," she says as much for her own benefit as Mai's. "Focus on the mission, and we'll all get home. Rich."

Mai's expression is unreadable. Born in the Company's advanced biotic creches and indoctrinated with the highest loyalty, duty has always guided Mai's service, not hazard pay. Nikela feels guilty. If she's forced to activate the failsafe, then Mai's dependable loyalty won't even matter.

3.

The bridge of *Convex Dissipation of Starlight* is as cramped as the rest of the vessel, with the tight, circular cabin nestled deep in the bulbous prow. There are no true windows, only virtual ports. Five acceleration couches ring a central display where a gridded representation of Crockett looms, surrounded by flickering orbital plots that march like ants.

The display ripples, straining to resolve the deformations of spacetime surrounding the planet. Crockett itself can't seem to hold shape, like a moon reflecting off the dark water of a deep well.

Three pairs of eyes turn to Lira as she enters the bridge. Two of the acceleration couches are empty—the navigator's and the captain's—and Abreu isn't on the bridge. Biotic engineer Choi grins at Lira from her couch. She's a dark, spindly woman made of elbows and sporting a spacer's buzzcut—a saints-damned shade of Abe. She recalls her old arguments with Abe about the attraction between synthetics and biotic engineers and realizes he may have been right.

Choi notices her bittersweet expression but misinterprets Lira's concerns.

"*Convex* can handle microjumps, no troubles at all," she drawls in a backwater Fort Arp accent. Choi exudes the cloying, chummy bravado of every soldier Lira's ever met. In that at least, she and Abe were different.

"I'm not troubled," Lira replies sulkily as she straps into the navigator's station.

"Don't let Choi rile you," says the officer next to her. Marca DuFour is the ship's technical engineer, in charge of all non-biotic systems. Her purple tonsure is strictly non-regulation, but Lira likes the brainy officer, even for the short time she's known her. She's a bit of a know-it-all though.

DuFour runs her fingers across her board, smiling as each status light winks to green.

"I double checked your figures, Lira. They're good. Great even." DuFour blushes and blurts, "Why you're not crewed to the best ships in the—"

Lira cuts the tech engineer off with a look. A know-it-all and a flirt. Another distraction she does not need.

The comms officer, an aggie named Speck, interrupts before DuFour can resume her patter.

"No comms traffic, naval or civilian," they say, worry lines creasing their brow. The comm shunt installed in their right temple cycles with soft amber lights. "Not even automated nav beacons."

"Keep scanning, Speck, but watch for those navy boats. We don't want to be caught with our asses in the air," Choi warns.

Lira frowns as she tunes her own display. A tangled knot of multicolored lines appears, the ship's best approximation of the quantum gradients flowing around the planet. A vortex of churning spacetime erupts from the south pole where the comet hit. She gasps. The gradients twist in violent, serpentine undulations, collapsing into the vortex. Lira reaches for the biotic interface. Maybe *Convex* can sniff its way through that thicket without getting trapped in the undertow.

The bridge hatch opens, and Captain Nikela Abreu steps through. Her face is tight, but she manages a smile.

"Sleep well, Navigator?"

"Fine," Lira replies, "but I wish I had more time to study these gradients."

Abreu's smile slips a little.

"Do your best," she says as she straps into her couch. "How's the ship, Choi?"

"Purring like a cat," the biotic specialist says. "We can go whenever Lira's ready."

"How about it, Lira?" the captain asks, tapping her stylus in the direction of the orbital display.

"The gradients are impossible for a world this size."

"You studied the report, yes, Lira?" Abreu asks, an eyebrow raised.

Lira closes her eyes and queries the biotic navigational feeds again, flushing. Of course, she read Abreu's sisterfucking report. But she'd normally expect these kinds of major inflection around a white dwarf or a neutron star, not a terrestrial planet like Crockett. *How is the planet even intact?*

In the tangle, she finds an endo-slope that might serve them well, a wobbling funnel of stability in the shifting coils of warped spacetime. A fringe of scabbed-over noise in its walls might be the patrol ships Choi mentioned, caught in a crushing probability shear. She sends them to the display for Abreu to see.

"Two Class III hazards breaking up in the tunnel wall. Our navy patrol?"

Abreu stares at the display for a moment before abruptly turning away, her expression unreadable. The rest of the crew are equally stone-faced. There were three hundred crew between those two ships, all so much quantum foam now.

The same fate could befall them.

"Why were they trying to get to the surface?" Choi wonders aloud.

"They were pulled in," Lira says darkly, strapping the navigation cuff around her wrist and thinking of her first encounter with the comet.

Lira's cuff opens a direct connection with the biotic core of *Convex*.

She'd sworn never to commune with a ship again after the infection of the systems on *Grass is Greener*. The severity of those probability shears mean she doesn't have much of a choice though.

As her mind melts into confluence with the ship, she realizes the biotic core of *Convex Dissipation of Starlight* is more aware of itself than *Grass* had been. *Convex* returns her mental touch with a soothing warmth and a confidence that mirrors Choi's bravado.

Hello, Lira, it seems to say. *Welcome home.*

And it does feel like home. Her own synapses flood with tingling joy as their designed purpose is once more fulfilled.

Thank you, Convex, she says, *are you ready for our journey?*

Lira shudders as *Convex* chirps another warning in her ear. It shows her something she didn't see on the sensor vanes before: thousands of biotic signals, pulsing on the surface of Crockett, a rippling quilt of color and light. She pauses, wondering what all those signals represented. New life on the dead planet?

Lira shudders.

One signal pulses with a warm rose glow from the eastern hemisphere, just north of the equator from a settlement designated AGC-10A. Cumberland Settlement. She's heard its melody before. As the signal touches her mind, the familiarity crystallizes into certainty.

Lira, it says. *How I've missed you.*

Abe? Abe!

Through the ship, Lira knows it's him, though she doesn't understand—or trust—*how* that could possibly be true. She held his hand while he died in his sleep. *Convex* quickly highlights another signal ten kilometers to the north of Abe at a storage complex. This one's familiar too, a cancerous thickening of green and black.

Pike.

"Lira?"

Captain Abreu's voice yanks her from her intimate dialog with the ship. Abreu leans close, her eyes narrowing in concern.

"Everything okay?"

Lira nods quickly. Maybe too quickly, judging from the wariness in Abreu's eyes.

"Adjusting stochastic balancing, sir," she says, and it's not a lie. Abreu's course has them heading straight for Pike. Setting down near Abe instead is well within the tolerances of the microjump though. Lira makes the necessary changes with the ship's help. Her heart thuds, but Abreu doesn't seem to notice her shaking hands. Given the gradients, the course will appear an acceptable deviation.

Lira activates the course on the central display. The countdown starts.

Thank you, she sends silently to *Convex*. The ship doesn't reply, deep in its own murmurs as it prepares to shunt to warp space. For some reason, the ship has conspired to reunite her with Abe.

For all the questions waiting to be answered on Crockett's surface, that one might be the greatest.

The ship's countdown reaches zero, and *Convex Dissipation of Starlight* shunts into warp space. Nikela rubs at the place where her warp cuff meets her wrist. She hasn't bothered to secure it. Staying awake is a risk, even for such a short jaunt, but there was something in her navigator's demeanor as she communed with the ship that Nikela didn't trust.

Nikela monitors the biotic core as the numbers kaleidoscope across her display. *Convex* slides right into the gradient tunnel, smooth as glass. Though her navigator has a history of fuckups, this run looks to be perfect. Too perfect maybe. The ship is set to exit warp right above their target.

There's a small tremble as *Convex* shunts back to real space, and the holo display once again shows Crockett, this time a swollen brown ball of rock looming mere kilometers before them. Nikela breathes a sigh of relief. Exit is surprisingly clean, and the warp inflection dissipates within normal tolerances. *Convex* floats safely below the distorted auroras of undulating spacetime, dropping steadily toward the landing zone. A sudden shock jolts through her.

They are off course.

Captain Nikela swears, wiping cold sweat from her brow. She reaches for the thruster override. Saints of shit, Lira fucked up the plot.

Nikela's anger spikes. She'd be willing to bet against all the Company's actuaries that the damned synthetic had changed course on purpose. The Company had picked up other signals on Crockett. *What if Lira detected one?*

Nikela fears she knows which signal she'd found: the Mistri anomaly. The only question is *how*? Those logs are encrypted. The display chirps. *Convex* plunges through the thick, phlegmy clouds that wreathe Crockett in a tattered blanket. Beneath them, the vast brown prairies unroll as far as Nikela can see. The wobbly line of the horizon smears back up into the sky. It hurts her eyes to look at it.

Below them, Cumberland Settlement rises from port when it should have risen from starboard. Nikela checks her display. There's a biotic pulse from deep within the town. Her anger grows and along with it a sense of inevitability.

Goddammit, of course it's the Mistri anomaly.

"What a dump," Choi mutters, blinking away hypersleep. The rest of the crew wake, yawning as they resume control of *Convex*. Lira opens her sapphire eyes, but she doesn't meet the captain's glare.

"We're off course, Navigator," Nikela says, steeling her tone against the strengthening tide of anxiety welling up within her. She's already got Pike to manage. The navigator's forcing her to deal with Mistri—her dad—far sooner than she'd planned.

Lira frowns guilelessly, checking her boards.

"But well within normal parameters, especially considering the quantum shear, Captain."

"Ten kilometers ain't so bad," Choi suggests, her Fort Arp accent slipping through. "And we've got the planetary hopper."

"Get the damn thing ready," Nikela grinds out through her teeth, ignoring Choi's puzzlement. Lira notices.

"My apologies, Captain" Lira whispers at Nikela's shoulder.

"Don't suckle my ass, Lira," she hisses back. "This isn't a mistake. This is treachery." Before she can say more, Speck interrupts.

"I-I'm picking up a message," the aggie shouts, confusion creasing their brow.

Icy water swirls in Nikela's guts. *Saints.*

"Let's hear it, Speck. Audio only," she quickly adds.

In a burst of static, a lone voice greets the crew. The tone is flat as if the speaker is just waking up.

"So. You've come."

Abraham Mistri's voice is like a fist in Nikela's stomach. She holds back the tears but only just. She clenches white-knuckled fists under her console.

Saints of sisterfucking shit. Not just an anomalous signal. It's Abraham Mistri. *Dad.*

Lira smiles. Her wide sapphire eyes shimmer with unshed but happy tears.

Dammit. Nikela attempts a sarcastic laugh, but it comes out an angry snort.

"Last I heard, you were on Oleander. Dead." she says. She clutches at her old anger, her bitterness. He'd abandoned her and her mom—so he'd been dead to her long before he'd died on Oleander. Whatever she's talking to now is just some sensor anomaly. A ghost.

Coordinates start flickering across the display. An address in Cumberland Settlement. Nikela breaks into another cold sweat. Lira stares at her curiously.

Nikela glares at Lira intently until she looks away, guilty.

"You and Lira . . . should come see me, Nikki. Before you do whatever else you came here to do."

Nikela feels the ice in her veins.

He knows about Pike. He knows what he is to me.

Nikela clenches her fists under her control board again until the angry tears subside. A cold rage is all that remains. Mistri doesn't get to come back from the dead. He doesn't get to swan into her life, not when she's on the verge of finding Pike after all this time.

Nikela decides to give the bastard something of what he wants, but she'll still leave Crockett with Pike as planned.

Dad—and Lira—be damned.

4.

Lira surveys the landscape from the wide boarding ramp of the *Convex*. A low pall of dust hugs the ground like a yellow fog. Biotic spores. The prairie is blanketed with patches of mold in hues of rust and old brass. Veins of electric blue and black thread through the diseased earth. The ground itself seems to strain upward, reaching into the yellow sky. The comet's legacy.

Her exosuit whines, the enviro filters kicking into overdrive. Lira hopes it will be enough. Even through the suit, she can almost feel the spores gathering on her skin.

AGC-10A, the Cumberland Settlement, looms to her left, its thick plascrete walls festooned with similar drifts of mold and other growths more akin to the coral found in Oleander's shallow seas. A massive gate pierces the wall, the open doors crusted by a lush garden of scintillating rainbow fungus. A handful of abandoned vehicles lie rotting before the gate: a combine, a cargo tread, and a patrol wheeler, all overgrown and sparkling.

Beyond lie the slab-sided factories and squat apartment blocks of Cumberland. No lights burn in the shadowed streets, though a faint green light pools on the sidewalks, cast from delicate traceries of biotic rot. It's a hideous landscape beyond anything she witnessed on *Grass is Greener*. Pike's mad ravings about Nameless Ones and alien paradises suddenly seem far too prescient.

"Keep those seals tight," Captain Abreu says as the rest of the exo-team assembles on the ramp. She glares at Lira. Lira glares back.

"You didn't tell me about Abe," she accuses the captain over the open channel.

"I didn't know," Abreu protests.

"I think you did."

"There were a lot of biotic signals," the captain admits. She switches to a private channel.

"Prophets' taint, Lira," she hisses, "don't you dare lecture me in front of my crew."

Lira continues to glare. There's something else in Abreu's eyes. Guilt. She's keeping more secrets. Lira's sure.

Choi interposes herself between them. Saints bless her.

"Captain, why'd we land *here*?"

"Ask Lira," Abreu retorts.

Lieutenant Mai and her six marines circle around them, and Lira tenses, realizing she's surrounded by grim-faced soldiers with pulse rifles. Mai's a synthetic, a combat model. Lira's outmatched. She takes three deep breaths and raises her hands, palms out.

"They won't shoot you," Abreu chuckles. "In fact, they'll keep you safe."

With a shuddering groan, a large section of the hull opens, and the planetary hopper wriggles out, lowering itself to the ground on spindly struts. Captain Abreu catches Mai's attention and gestures to the hopper. She turns back to Lira.

"Safe from what?"

"Abraham Mistri. I'm sending you and Choi to talk to Dad while I complete my assignment."

She sounds more resigned than angry. It surprises Lira.

"Don't you want to see him?"

Abreu shakes her head. "We said our goodbyes long before you did. After the mission? We'll see."

"He's dangerous," Lira warns, not talking about Abe. "I thought you wanted me along."

"I'm not sure I can trust you. And now we have two problems. It's better you go see Mistri."

Lira's pulse quickens at the thought of seeing Abe again, even if he isn't real. Her misgivings about Pike threaten to boil over though, spoiling the reunion.

Mai steps up to the captain, her expression is hidden behind her suit's faceplate.

"We should depart, Captain," Mai says to Abreu. Four of the marines file aboard the hopper. Two remain with Choi.

Abreu turns to follow Mai. Lira calls after her.

"This can turn to shit in an instant," she warns the captain.

Abreu waves in acknowledgment. "Noted, Lira. We'll keep the comms open. Tell 'Dad' hi." Abreu and Mai vanish into the squat, bug-eyed hopper.

Lira sighs and turns to Choi. "My warning goes double for you," she says, trying to ignore the old shake in her hands.

"Don't worry," Choi says, misinterpreting her anxiety and tapping her sidearm. "I know how biotic engineers think. I can handle Mistri."

Lira blanches, a cold uncertainty settling in her artificial bones. She hadn't considered the possibility that Abe would turn violent. He isn't—*wasn't*—that kind of man. *But then,* Lira admits to herself, *she doesn't really know who—or what—really waited for them in that Cumberland hab-tower.*

As the hopper bounces into the sky, Lira and her team pass through the gate into the settlement. The narrow streets swallow them up, and even the soldiers' comm chatter is muted. They pass under fungal lattices of purple and yellow fibers, past hummocks of rot that might once have been animals. Or colonists. Abreu had insisted that everyone had been evacuated, but Lira isn't so sure now. Some of those hummocks have arms and legs.

Choi walks beside her, pistol unholstered. Their escorts walk one ahead, one behind, occasionally scanning the street with the muzzles of their pulse rifles. Both women are twitchy with nerves, and Lira finds herself flinching every time they sweep her way.

Choi is distressingly chipper as they travel deeper into the corrupted settlement. With an ever-present grin, she runs a wand-like scanner over every patch of biotic corruption inside two meters.

"Virgin's taint, Lira, I ain't ever seen growth like this, not even inside a ship's core." She pauses in front of a bulbous cluster, like gigantic, oozing grapes that might once have been a cooling pump or a screaming survivor.

"Didn't they brief you on *Grass is Greener*?" she asks the engineer. Abreu's crew seems oddly uninformed about their assignment.

"Some holos," Choi replies. "Ain't nothing in comparison to this."

The engineer goes silent for a long stretch. Lira can guess what she's thinking.

"You grow up here?" Lira says as they walk past the husk of a loader-bot, its tentacles crusted with fungal blossoms.

Choi cuts her eyes at Lira, her grin vanished. "Yeah, but up north. Near Fort Arp. Wasn't no settlement as big and fancy as this. We didn't have walls, for one."

Lira nods. Facilities like AGC-10A were built in the wake of AgriGrow Corporation's consolidation efforts, the sort of large-scale industrialization that put small farmers out of business.

"Our farm was outside of town, and you could see for kilometers around. All that golden wheat-sedge rippling in the wind." Choi's gaze turns wistful.

"I'm sorry, Choi. Abe and I once dreamed about settling down here too. Starting up a farm of our own. But even before the comet fell, we decided to get as far fucking away from Crockett as we could get."

Choi grunts, fingering the butt of her pistol. "You think it's really Mistri that's waiting for us?"

"Something of him, at least."

"He died," Choi counters.

"In my arms," Lira says.

"So it can't *be* him."

How to explain the biotic contagion of Crockett's comet to Choi? Did she even know how it changed Pike? "Whatever he is, I'm willing to listen to what he has to say."

Choi grins sadly, the tension in her face easing. "I think you just want another chance to say goodbye."

Saints, she's right. But Lira says nothing.

The street splits at a Y-junction, the main road continuing past a row of collapsed shops and public utility booths. A smaller street to the left winds around low-slung sheds and processing fabs to the main entrance of a hab-tower. The structure is oddly free from much of the biotic rot.

"This is it," Lira says as her suit chimes. Her hands tremble again.

Choi places a hand on her shoulder and squeezes warmly. "For what it's worth, Lira, I'd be going bonkers right now if I were in your boots. But we got your back."

"Thanks," Lira replies, feeling guilty after her navigational deception on *Convex*.

Choi, flanked by the watchful pair of soldiers, marches straight up to the door. She retrieves a scrambler from a suit pouch and clamps it on the lock pad. The door pops open with a clang Lira feels through the faceplate of her helmet. Her mouth goes dry.

"Hello?" Choi broadcasts on speaker into the entry vestibule.

Thready yellow webs of fungus hang curtain-like between the vestibule and the atrium. A glow suffuses the air, a curious pale light originating from nowhere and everywhere all at once.

There's a flicker, a whisper of noise. Choi jabs her pistol at the receding dark.

"Come out of there!" she shouts.

"Don't shoot. I'm harmless," an amused voice calls back. A tingle starts creeping up Lira's spine.

Before Choi or the marines can stop her, Lira pushes through the fungal curtains into the atrium. Once the space had served as a common area: a few storefronts and a café ringed a now-dry fountain. Rainbow mold grows everywhere in familiar tendrils of fleshy rot.

But suit or no, her breath catches in her throat. The tingle moves up her back and out across her limbs.

Abe sits at a café table as if he'd been waiting on her to show up for a date. He wears no exosuit, only simple engineer's coveralls. Abe looks fifteen years younger than when he died and, despite the overgrown jungle of biotic infection growing around him, as if he'd just stepped off *Grass is Greener*.

His kind eyes brim with tears, and his warm smile electrifies Lira.

"Lira!" he cries, standing.

Tears blur the apparition of her beloved. It's impossible, but Abe's alive, standing before her, arms wide.

She can stand it no longer. Lira races across the atrium and takes Abe Mistri into her arms.

5.

The hopper's autopilot sets them down hard. Nikela is nearly thrown from her bench as the craft rocks to a halt. Mai and her marines exchange glances. Normally, the hopper touches down with the grace of the insect it resembles. Nikela makes a note to have Choi and DuFour inspect the craft once they're back aboard *Convex*.

The sight out the porthole is enough to mollify her annoyance. A row of dark towers crowds the banks of a dry riverbed. Grain silos. Nikela checks the datatab on her wrist. Their objective is inside.

Nikela's anxious. Part of it is simply the mission jitters, but who she's going after has a lot to do with how she's feeling. Lira's warning hangs over her too. *Shit in an instant.*

But saints, Nikela's far more prepared than Lira and her ferry crew ever were. She knows what they might face. They have weapons. And the failsafe.

As if reading her thoughts, Mai looks at her expectantly. With a twinge of guilt, Nikela signals the order to embark. The lieutenant and her four marines sling their weapons and hustle out of the airlock and onto the surface of Crockett without hesitation. Good soldiers.

Mai approaches as Nikela exits the airlock, gesturing to the grain storage complex. Fuzzy puffballs drift in the air between them. Nikela checks the seals on her suit. Still green.

"Captain, do you see that?"

At first, Nikela thinks the merc means the puffballs and the three-meter-high fingerlike purple tubercles that emit them. They look like inside-out lungs, coughing in a perpetual miasma. She follows the muzzle of Mai's plasma rifle instead toward the base of the closest silo.

Nikela reflexively brings her gloved hand to her mouth, bumping her fingers on her helmet. The other four marines mutter over the comms at the sight.

Saints of shit.

The foundations of each silo are slicked in an inky slime so black it makes her eyes ache. She glances away, surprised at purplish afterimages of the goo as if she'd just stared into the sun too long. But is it her retinas that waver or the air around the slime?

"Keep back, Lieutenant," she warns as Mai creeps a step closer to the silo.

"Not to worry, sir," she replies. "Just nudging my helmet sensors into range. That slime's emitting slight radioactivity."

Nikela wishes she could measure quantum gradients with her suit. She had her suspicions about that radioactivity.

"Can we enter the complex?" Their suits can handle hard radiation but not quantum shear.

Mai nods. "As long as we're out quick."

Nikela orders them into the complex, keeping to the relative safety of the paved, fungus-ridden walkway. The foul slime drips from the entrance, puddling at the threshold. The exosuit crackles radiation warnings as a chill crawls under Nikela's suit. Pike called them here. It must be safe. She takes a deep breath and steps over the puddle into the complex.

Mai and the marines keep in formation around her. Nikela appreciates the protection. She'll recommend bonus hazard pay.

As they approach the largest of the silos, Nikela flashes on a memory from when she was eight years old. Dad yelling at her to watch out for plume lizards as she splashes into a creek in the jungle ravine that ran behind their house on Oleander. He was worried about her of course, but those were happier times overall. Her dad had been content servicing biotic desalinization plants, his desperate love for the biotic cores of starships and synthetics still years away from blooming.

It's not that Nikela begrudged his passion for those things. She's a *starship* captain after all. It's how he lied about being happy at home while she grew up. Happy with her mom. Happy with her. And then he left.

Happy times are an illusion. Nikela has never forgotten that lesson.

You must love being around all this biotic growth, old man, she thinks uncharitably. They stop short of the massive gray tower.

It's supported by an exoskeleton of processing machinery and the, by now, familiar tangle of biotic rot. Fraying wheat sacks lay stacked against the foundation. All the bags have split open, vomiting their slimy black contents. Out of the corner of Nikela's eyes, the ground itself billows like an ocean swell. She closes her eyes until the dizziness passes.

Her suit grinds out another warning, this time identifying the source of the trouble. Virgin's taint, it's the *wheat-sedge* that's radioactive. Warping spacetime. *At least there are no venomous plume lizards,* she chuckles to herself.

Nikela toggles her faceplate through several filters until she finds one that keeps her eyes from hurting when she looks at the slime. It cuts her peripheral vision, but at least she doesn't see the ground dancing like waves at the corners of her eyes.

"Switch to visor three. Match my settings," she orders the company. There's a chorus of beeps in her ears as her soldiers obey. Nikela pauses, wondering whether she should enter the silo or try to draw Pike out.

She switches to broadcast, still undecided what to say to him.

"Pike? We're here. We received your signal. Come on out and talk?"

The only reply is the click of their suits' dosimeters. Another wave of dizziness hits. Nikela steadies herself against the remains of a cargo crate, hoping Mai doesn't notice.

The synthetic is carefully watching the entrance to the big silo.

"I guess we go in," Nikela says. She isn't even sure what she's looking for now. Surely Pike won't just be sitting there waiting with a cup of tea. She takes a step. Mai blocks her with an outstretched arm.

"I won't let you go in, sir," she says. "Not until I clear the structure."

"Nothing's clear here," Nikela says as the merc's silhouette shimmers like a heat mirage. She shakes her head. Mai gives her a strange look. *Shit in an instant.*

"Are you okay, sir?" Mai asks.

"I'm fine. Take Sun and Davey in with you," Nikela relents. "Ten meters only and report what you see."

Mai nods, gesturing to the other soldiers to follow. Davey hefts her rifle and marches smartly behind her CO, but Sun shoots a nervous look at Nikela, the fear visible in her brown eyes, even beneath her polarized faceplate.

Saints, they all saw me stumble. Didn't they feel it too?

Nikela glares at Sun until she double-times after Mai. The trio of mercs switch on their helmet lights, vanishing into the darkened silo.

Nikela turns away from the two remaining soldiers, squeezing her eyes shut until her face hurts. The pain makes the lightheadedness pass. She swallows her fear until it's nothing but an icy stone in her gut. She breathes in the long moments until Mai breaks her comm silence.

"Captain, it's a mess in here," the lieutenant reports.

"I need more than that, Mai," Nikela snaps more impatiently than she'd meant.

There's a few more seconds of Mai breathing, followed by the glimmer of a helmet light from within the silo.

"There's more rotting grain in here. A *lot* of it. And there are other . . . plants . . . growing from the mulch pile. Purple bulbs like some sort of seaweed. Air toxicity is high, but the radiation is about the same. Can you tell me what we're supposed to be looking for?"

Nikela sighs. Given the invitation, she'd hoped Pike would make himself more obvious.

"A survivor," she says. "A man in his seventies. I'll send the file—"

"Wait," Mai says, cutting her off. "There's something dangling up high. Caught on the machinery. Light can't quite reach—"

Screams erupt over the comms. Sun's. Staccato bursts of plasma fire strobe the interior of the silo. The marines' silhouettes dance with a larger shadow, one made of spikes and lashing tendrils.

The pair of marines with Nikela take up defensive stances.

"We're going in," she yells. She doesn't wait for them to reply as she dashes in.

Nikela's suit ticks a frantic warning as she crosses the threshold. The floor seems to tilt sideways, and she slumps against the doorframe as her marines charge past. Plasma fire rips the air. Nikela wants to shut her eyes against the strobing light and the wildly tilting ground. One of the marines—Davey—flies up into the blackness of the silo, screaming. Her suit's telemetry goes silent, and she doesn't come back down.

Sun slumps against the curved interior wall, motionless. Mai stands her ground, swinging the muzzle of her rifle, tracing the outline of a monstrous form with her gunfire.

Nikela's helmet adjusts to the lighting conditions, and she finally sees it: a gigantic vegetal horror composed of wriggling black fibers, each the thickness of her arm. Purplish flowers bud along the length of those tendrils, oozing a greenish pus. Meter-long bony spines ring the crown of the mass. Nikela recognizes them from the holo.

Pike?

Saints of shit, she can smell him, despite her suit, an ammoniac reek crashes into her, bringing new waves of dizziness. The monstrosity moves with inhuman speed, even faster than Mai. The synthetic unloads a whole magazine of plasma bolts into the creature, tearing out gloppy, smoking chunks. It smacks her with a hideous appendage, and she flies into the wall.

In a sudden panic, Nikela empties her own pistol into the Pike-creature. She smirks as its purple flowers blister and ooze, blasted apart. The other pair of marines join in, pouring on plasma bolts until its great bulk shudders to the earth and stills.

Nikela pants, breathing a sigh of relief when Mai gets to her feet. She walks shakily over to where Sun lies crumpled. The poor marine's faceplate was shattered by a biotic spine. There's not much left inside the helmet. Nikela's grateful she can't see what's left of Sun's face.

"Prophet's asshole," Mai says. "It got Davey too. What the fuck is that thing, Captain?"

Nikela edges closer to the vile corpse of the biotic creature. Saints of shit, she hadn't wanted to kill him. She can't decide if she feels the same after what just happened.

"Pretty sure it's Durance Pike," she coughs, still smelling ammonia in her helmet.

But she'd wanted Pike alive. She *needed* to talk to him; she had so many questions. But answers could come from the dead too, and there was still a 25 percent bonus in the offing.

Virgin's taint, maybe she'd have to talk to Abraham Mistri after all. Then they could get the hell off this sisterfucking planet.

As if the ferry incident had never happened, Abe studies Lira from across the café table, his hand in hers. His brown eyes are, as ever, soft and kind. That cherished smile plays at the corners of his mouth as Lira works up the nerve to ask, "Is it really you, Abe?"

He nods, but a sadness creeps into his eyes. "It is. And isn't. I think you understand, my love."

"No?" But maybe she can guess.

"*Grass is Greener*. It sampled me. Stored me. Recreated me. I'm biotic like you, Lira. It *is* me talking to you. I think, I feel, I worry about you. I love you."

Lira sucks in a ragged breath to hide how much it hurts to hear those words again after so sisterfucking long. She finds her hands trembling again. The contagion that had killed her ship—and so many of its crew—gave Abe back. There's no stimbulb in existence that could calm her now.

"You . . . died on Oleander five years ago. Was that you too?"

Abe looks apologetic.

"The sampling took something of me away. I recall those years on Oleander though. Like looking through a hazy fog. Somehow all my selves are connected."

Lira clenches her jaw. *Connected?* She'd never forget his decline in those years, his failing body, his absent mind. *Had part of him already been here?* "Saints of shit, Abe," she chokes, "you spent the last year in a coma. I didn't even get to say goodbye."

Abe's eyes shine with tears too, but shadows deepen in his expression.

"Why *are* you here, Lira? You shouldn't be. It's dangerous."

She frowns. "You asked me to come."

"Only after I sensed you in orbit."

Lira frowns. What to tell him of Abreu and her fool's mission? What to tell him of his estranged daughter? What to tell him of how *Convex* showed him to her? "I was hired on by a crew to break the quarantine. I think they're military black ops or a very well-funded corporate retrieval team."

Abe's eyebrow notches up. He scratches the top of his head with slender fingers. "Retrieval, eh?"

Lira nods, deciding she has to trust him about the mission. "Abe. They're here for Pike. Or whatever's left of him."

The news sends a flash of anger across Abe's placid face.

Lira shudders. The last time she'd seen that look on Abe's face was when they huddled in the weapons locker aboard the stricken *Grass is Greener*, discussing how to take Pike down. *What isn't* this *Abe saying?*

"They're idiots, but maybe we can get you out of here too," Lira insists. He could tell her everything when they were off Crockett. When they were safe.

Abe shakes his head. "And go back to Oleander? I'm afraid not, Lira."

"I'm sure they'll want to bring you—"

Abe's sad eyes tell Lira all she needs to know.

"You can't leave," she says.

"That's right. And now that I'm awake, I have duties. Responsibilities."

Responsibilities to what, Lira wonders.

"On *Grass is Greener*, Pike ranted about a new paradise and Nameless Ones bullshit. Is this what he meant?" She can't quite keep the acid from her tone as she gestures at the curtains of biotic slime hanging in the atrium.

Abe's expression turns serious again, but he looks more resigned than angry. "I'm not sure this is exactly what he had in mind."

Lira thinks he is telling the truth, but something still seems off. She glares at him, hoping he'll open up.

Abe releases her hand and steeples his fingers as if in prayer. He looks past her to Choi and the marines, shuffling uneasily in the atrium's entrance arch.

"I know this much, Lira. Crockett was dying before the comet," Abe says, meeting her gaze. "The Blight. Pike had the right of *that*, I suppose. Crops and people, more dying every year. There's new life now."

"But what kind, Abe? 'Nameless Ones'?" Lira laughs, but an icy fear takes hold in her root. Pike couldn't be right about that, could he?

Abe shrugs. "Sacred life, Lira. Vibrant life. But it must remain here for some time yet to be nurtured. To grow. When things are ready, it will return to space."

"They won't wait," she tells him. "They're intending to take Pike now."

Abe's eyes are haunted, and there's a flash of anguish across his face. "Ah, that's why Nikki's really here. I should have known it wasn't to see me."

Lira frowns. "What happened between you two? And why didn't you tell me you had a daughter?"

"Saints, Lira, you kept what happened on *Highline* from me for years. Don't begrudge me my secrets." Abe sounds bitter. He lets out a long sigh, stirring fungal puffballs from the table. "And there's more, I'm afraid. See, Nikki is my daughter by adoption. Her mother found other lovers when I was . . . less attentive. Durance Pike, for one."

Abe's admission drives the breath from Lira's synthetic lungs. She almost doesn't notice when her suit picks up the ghost of a signal on the priority channel, a scrambled order from Abreu to her marines. Shrill, electric screams echo through her comms.

It's the discharge of plasma rifles.

6.

Durance Pike hadn't been much of a father to Nikela Mistri Abreu, far less than even Abraham Mistri had. Mom had always been susceptible to rustic charms and a rural accent. She'd had a few partners to ease the loneliness when Abe was away. Durance Pike was one. He sent money sometimes, but her mom only told her where the windfalls came from after Abe had left for good: the man who raised her wasn't the man who fathered her.

As she grew, Nikela became determined to find Pike. With backbreaking effort, she entered the ranks of the Company, hoping its considerable resources would help her track him down. She learned he'd worked for them as a strikebreaker and black-bag agent for a time. Then he'd aged out. Retired. Vanished.

It was the Company's version of the truth, but Nikela had ferreted out the secret files that tracked his movements afterward. Detailed his involvement with the eschatological Gray Temple cult and the enigmatic Brother Hong.

When he turned up in the passenger manifest of the ferry *Grass is Greener* along with Nikela's adopted father—*and* his latest lover—well, destiny sure seemed to be drawing her to Pike at last. He'd died on that doomed ship, she'd thought.

Then came the holo transmission from Crockett, seemingly tailored for her. Destiny indeed.

Nikela hopes Pike is somehow still alive in all that goo and starts sawing into the fleshy, net-like fibers of the biotic creature's skin with her electrostatic knife, careful not to stab too deeply just in case.

"Captain?" Mai asks. The surviving pair of soldiers watch nervously as Nikela chops at the ropey husk.

Nikela glances at her slime-slicked gloves. She's preoccupied, still shaky from the firefight. She carves into the creature like a holiday goat, desperately hoping that Pike is in there. Black, fibrous tumors part before her crackling blade, filled with a blue-green pus. Nikela's suit's filters glow amber, but the seals hold. A sudden gleam of white in the mass rewards her efforts.

Saints of shit, she's right. She tugs on the fleshy limb. It's an arm. A human arm.

"Virgin's taint," Mai gasps.

Nikela tugs on the arm, excitement growing. It's attached to a hairless but very human torso. A whole body. He's young, this reborn Pike. *This is how Mom knew him,* Nikela thinks.

Nikela drags him out of the cancerous biotic mass, propping him next to poor Davey. His chest rises and falls. His baby-smooth skin glows with a lustrous vitality. His eyes flutter open. They are soft and blue. Nikela suppresses tears of joy. She's fucking done it. She's found Pike. *Father.*

"I thought we were looking for biotic seeds," Mai says, confused. Her part of the mission brief had been considerably less specific. There's a whole sea of misgivings in the lieutenant's troubled face.

"And we found one." Nikela can't repress her tears now. He's perfect. She can see herself in his youthful face, the same studied intensity in his eyes, the determined set of his jaw. Her superiors will be happy. She'll get commendations, at least two. But the money and awards are secondary victories.

"Who is that?" Mai asks. "He looks familiar somehow."

"Durance Elphonse Pike," Nikela says, smiling.

Mai steadies her grip on her rifle.

"He killed two of our marines," she says flatly.

Pike regards Mai and Nikela like a wary animal. Mai's reminder blunts her curious excitement at the reunion. She hopes she hasn't made a mistake.

"Durance Pike. I'm captain Nikela Mistri Abreu of the packet ship *Convex Dissipation of Starlight*. We're going to take you home."

Pike gawps like a fish, sucking for breath. He emits a wretched gasp, trying to form words.

Nikela pats him reassuringly on the shoulder. He's warm. Solid. Human.

"I don't—" he sucks for air as if his lungs have never worked before. He frowns, furrowing his brow as if trying to remember something.

Nikela tries to reassure him. "It's okay. We have medics on our ship."

Pike shakes his head, and his expression turns awed. He speaks once more, this time his words even and clear. "I don't. Believe it."

Nikela laughs despite herself. *Believe what? That someone would come? He'd asked for help. What had he expected?* "We're the only way off world, I'm afraid, Pike. But trust me when I—"

His mouth splits into an unsettling smile full of perfect teeth. He surges to his feet, gazing down at her, eyes sparking with joy despite his aggressive stance.

Mai raises her rifle in alarm, but Pike ignores it.

"I don't believe it. You look just like her," he crows.

"Like who," Nikela says, a sudden flutter in her chest. *Mom. He means Mom.*

Pike's answer catches her off guard.

"You look like *Mama*," he says, laughing. "I promised her that I'd plant the seeds!"

Nikela stumbles back in surprise. *Seeds?* Pike reaches out to catch her, a mixture of victory and concern on his face. Mai misinterprets his gesture and jams her rifle into his ribs.

"Back away, or I will shoot," she warns.

Pike turns to glare at Mai, a dangerous defiance kindling in his blue eyes. He moves *much* faster than Lieutenant Mai's trigger finger.

The gunfire on the comms draws the two soldiers through the hab entryway and back out into the street. Choi remains in the atrium with Lira and Abe, her posture rigid.

"Captain! Status report," she shouts into the comm. There's no reply.

"What's going on, old man?" Choi demands, thrusting her pistol at Abe.

He shrugs. "Seems Nikki found who she was looking for," he replies.

Lira stands between Abe and Choi, glaring down at him. "You knew about Nikki. About Pike. All along," Lira accuses him. "When that bastard was poisoning *Grass is Greener*—your sisterfucking ship—you didn't tell me then?"

Abe shakes his head. "I knew later, Lira. *After*. It's complicated—"

Lira cuts him off with a jab of her hand, fighting a wave of queasiness as she remembers what happened on *Grass is Greener*. "No. I can't hear this right now."

More gunfire chatters through the comms.

"Sir!" one of their escorts shouts. "Davey's flatlined. Sun too."

"Virgin's taint," mutters Choi, one foot toward the door. She signals *Convex* and switches to a secure channel. Lira can't hear what she's saying to the crew back on the ship.

Lira moves toward her, glancing back at Abe. She can't trust him. Could she ever?

"You and Mistri stay here," Choi says on the open channel. "He'll only complicate things."

"You're not facing Pike without me," Lira says, still glaring at Abe.

"You. Ain't. Coming," Choi insists, her drawl slipping out with her anger.

"She's right," Abe says to Choi. "We should go with you." His brown eyes are shadowed with grief.

"We can't trust you," Lira counters.

Choi lowers her pistol. "We can't trust *you* either, Lira."

Lira sighs, trying to appear as calm as possible. Every second they stayed here was a second of opportunity lost. Choi seems uncertain. She likes Lira, maybe she'd listen.

"Choi, what do you know about Durance Pike?"

"Nothing really. And there're NDAs for the little bit I do. They'll know if I break them."

The crackle of gunfire ceases, and an ominous silence descends over the comms.

"Who will know? The navy?" She says the last sarcastically. There's no way this is a navy operation.

Choi grimaces again. She switches to a direct channel with Lira.

"You know it ain't them," she admits, her tone conspiratorial.

"Then tell me who."

Choi takes a deep breath, and her voice shakes.

"What I can say, my mission brief detailed the retrieval of a seed. Something of this place to study. I guess that could be Pike."

Lira goes cold. Saints of shit. That's a very bad idea.

"That's incredibly stupid, Choi. You know what kind of seeds grow here."

Lira can't help but look at Abe when she says it.

Choi shrugs. "Maybe. But if we don't do it, they'll send someone who will."

"Who will send them?"

Gunfire rips through the comms again. Mai's suit shows signs of containment breach.

Choi shuts her mouth and looks pleadingly into Lira's eyes. "Please. Stay here," she orders Lira. "We'll come back for you. I promise."

Lira doesn't doubt Choi's sincerity, but there are no guarantees in this mess. She won't be left behind. She drops her shoulder and rushes the engineer. She's no combat model synthetic, but she's still fast, and Choi isn't a true marine. She rams into Choi's solar plexus. If they survive the afternoon, her shoulder will hurt for days. The biotic engineer staggers back and drops her pistol from her nerveless fingers, gasping.

Lira scoops up the weapon. She secures the safety, aiming the muzzle at the dirt.

"I'm not going to hurt you, Choi. I happen to like engineers." She jerks her chin back to Abe, who grins faintly. "But we're losing time arguing."

Choi gasps to catch her wind back. Her eyes are red with a mix of betrayal and terror.

Abe approaches Lira. "You both should get back to *Convex* and run like hell," he warns. "But you won't, will you?"

Lira shakes her head.

Abe chuckles. "You're loyal to your crew up until the end, Lira."

"You're coming with us, Abe."

Even after all those years planet-bound on Oleander, she's still a spacer. She has a responsibility to any crew she serves with, even this one. And Abe is still part of her crew, no matter how Crockett has changed him.

He sets his hands on her shoulders as if to embrace her. Through the haptics, she can feel his hands, warm and strong. She flinches even as she hungers for his touch. One by one, her faceplate displays wink out until all she can see is Abe's lean face staring back at her, his gaze bittersweet.

"I wish we had more time, my love," he says, "but this is what we have."

"Abe?" Tears sting her eyes. Lira feels as if she's on a precipice about to leap into the unknown. Abe's touch grows heavier. Her suit chimes a power warning, and for a moment, she fears it will fail.

To her relief, her displays flare to life once more, and all systems show nominal status. Abe releases her. The atrium rattles with the roar of starship engines. *Convex* approaching.

"Let's go help Nikki," Abe says. "I owe her that much."

Lira cocks her head in confusion. "But what about Pike?"

Abe smiles. "We'll help him too."

Durance Pike had been an assassin and mercenary in his first life. From the efficient way he dispatches her soldiers, Nikela realizes rebirth has not affected those skills. He's even deadlier now, stronger. She dives from him as he delivers precise, brutal jabs, tearing through the vulnerable systems of their exosuits with his bare hands. Mai scrambles back, trying to get a clear shot at Pike.

Expressionless, Pike rounds on the marine lieutenant, grappling the muzzle of her rifle and tearing it from her grip.

"Pike, leave her alone!"

Saints of fucking shit, this is not the reunion she imagined. *She was sisterfucking naive,* she admits to herself as the blood runs cold in her veins.

"Father!" she shouts in desperation.

Mai's violet eyes go wide, glancing at her as Pike closes in. He ignores Nikela's pleading.

Nikela raises her pistol, trying to get a clear shot at him, though she still doesn't want to shoot. It might be the only way to get his attention.

That or the failsafe.

"Mai! Code Void Gamma Two!" Nikela shouts the order.

Mai stiffens as the Company's secret protocols rewire her synthetic brain. Somehow the marine stays just out of Pike's reach, but her violet eyes are blank. Nikela feels a fleeting pang of guilt. *This is the damned mission on the line,* she reminds herself. *It's this, or we're all dead. Mai will understand.*

Pike does hesitate. He pants, his pale skin slick with exertion as he scans Mai with a hard gaze. Nikela breathes a little easier. He can sense the failsafe. He knows what's at stake. Maybe he'll listen now. It's a short-lived hope.

"That's not the way to a new world, Nikela," he chides. "We must separate the grain from the chaff."

Pike lunges once more at Mai.

Mai's recovered from her failsafe activation, though her eyes have turned a milky blue. She slams an armored fist into Pike's head, and teeth spray from his dangling jaw. Her Company training takes over. She delivers a vicious kick that drives him to the moldy earth. Mai screams as she unsheathes her electrostatic knife and buries it in his exposed back. She meets Nikela's eyes with a cold glare of her own as she thrusts the knife deeper into Pike's back, sawing through muscle and bone. She knows her captain has betrayed her. She's not happy about it.

Nikela doesn't want Pike to die, but what choice does she have now? Mai might come for her next. *Saints of shit, maybe I deserve Mai's vengeance.*

But Pike's not defeated so easily. He roars to his feet, tossing Mai aside with a sweep of his sinewy arms. The marine staggers on her feet, stunned by his sudden strength. Nikela feels a strange sense of victory.

Pike plows into Mai again, hacking savagely at her with the edges of his naked hands. His first strike deadens a nerve cluster, and her right arm dangles limply. The next cracks the housing of her exosuit's control panel, shattering the sensor plates. A third blow catches a breathing hose, shearing it from its helmet coupling. As she wrestles with Pike, Mai inhales a cloud of black spores. Her gurgling breaths fill the comms as she topples, Pike on top of her. He continues to tear her apart.

The violence rips Nikela from her paralysis. *Goddammit, whose side am I on?*

Nikela raises her pistol with a shaking hand. She aims for the ES knife still lodged hilt-deep in Pike's back and flicks the pistol to full-auto. Pulls the trigger. Black-red flowers of flesh and bone blossom between his shoulders. For an instant, the spray of tissue creates a macabre illusion of spreading wings.

Pike doesn't seem to notice. The wounds on his shoulders pucker shut, dribbling a milky biotic ooze. He digs into Mai's suit with clawlike fingers. Into her chest.

Oh saints, no.

"Alright, child," Pike gasps as Mai stops moving. "You want apocalypse, I'll give it to you."

A warning bleats in Nikela's comms. The failsafe. *Saints of shit, the failsafe is activating without her command.* The failsafe is a bomb, of course, a spacetime warp charge with a point seven-five gradient, enough to shunt half a continent into a hyperdense chunk of matter the size of her fist. Nothing could survive that, not even Pike. He's calling her bluff.

Nikela holds down the trigger, sprays him with the full magazine of her pistol. Plasma bolts rip through her pseudo-father's ghastly flesh. He wheels on Nikela too late. As his ruined jaw knits itself back to his skull, he frowns.

"I promised Brother Hong. I promised Mama. I made this world for *you*, daughter-captain," he groans. "Why do you reject it?"

In answer, Nikela thumb-selects a high-explosive charge and fires. The plasma round crackles through the air, punching through his face before exploding. A mist of blood and gristle patter to the floor. What's left of Pike topples to the ground.

So much for family reunions. Nikela will grieve what she's lost when there's time.

Nikela crawls to Mai. The marine is fighting for breath in the toxic atmosphere. Her helmet is shattered, and her mouth is stained black from the biotic contagion. Clear biotic blood leaks from her crushed chest, glistening in the weird afternoon light.

"You . . . hid the warp bomb . . . from my diagnostics." Mai seems more puzzled than hurt. That makes Nikela feel worse somehow.

"Lieutenant. Mai. I'm sorry—"

She holds the woman's hand as Mai chokes on her own synthetic blood.

"I can't stop it," Mai gasps.

Nikela peers into the ruin of Mai's thoracic cavity, wincing. The whirling gyros of the warp bomb's casing are visible beneath the ruined tissue, nestled between Mai's organoceramic ribs. The starlight glow of spacetime surrounds them like a halo.

"Pike's dead. We'll get you back to *Convex*. Patch you up."

Mai's a valuable asset in the field and even a friend. Nikela will make sure that the marine gets the best care even if it comes out of her own pay.

Mai shakes her head, her eyes wide with terror.

"Not dead. Life signs."

What?

Nikela starts as her exosuit pings back a positive signal from his body.

Cellular respiration.

Heat.

Movement.

Pike's fingers twitch, reaching for something. Reaching for *her*.

Tendrils of flesh bud from the ragged stump of his neck. They unfurl into flowers of sinew, bone, and teeth. Pike nods the stump of his head, and the warp bomb chimes once more, this time deactivating. Mai goes still.

"Crockett blooms again," Pike drawls. His voice oozes up like honeyed sap from the fleshy blossoms.

Nikela shudders as he reaches out to her, purplish nails glinting in the wan yellow light. She tries to run, but a strange paralysis holds her. Her finger twitches on the trigger of her pistol, but she can't quite pull it. The magazine's nearly depleted. One charge left.

"We'll walk together in our garden. Your mama would be happy to see us two here." His mane of petals folds around the stump of his neck, remolding themselves in a semblance of Pike's face with a lipless smile. Vegetal buds like eyes flick toward the sky. "Maybe she's even up there somewhere, watching over us."

Nikela wants to scream, but her mouth is as frozen as her feet. Her skin crawls. She imagines microscopic tendrils from Pike, from Crockett, reaching through the soles of her boots, digging into her flesh. Horror crescendos in fresh waves of dizziness. The ammoniac stink fills her helmet.

Pike holds up his right hand. His fingers elongate, stretching into purplish spikes.

"We got the same genes, kid. We grew up out of the soil of Crockett despite the Blight. You belong here."

"Sisterfucker," she stammers, cracking through the ice of her terror. Her trigger finger twitches.

He looks hurt, the corners of his mouth turning down.

A long black tendril uncoils from Pike's spine, a single ropey limb like those that had encased him when he'd first appeared in the silo.

"Don't fight it, Nikela. I can help you see if you'll let me."

"I see plenty," Nikela snarls, squeezing the trigger and discharging the last explosive round in the chamber. Pike's still smiling when his malformed head explodes in an oil slick of biotic gore.

What's left of Pike thrashes on the soiled earth, and Nikela knows she doesn't have much time before he reforms. The failsafe. She has to reactivate it. There's no time to warn the rest of the crew of *Convex*.

No time left at all.

Nikela staggers toward Mai, careful to keep far from Pike's twitching corpse. She queries the warp bomb. It responds with sluggish awareness, but the remote timer refuses to activate. She leans over the fallen marine. There's a manual detonator on the bomb's casing. Her fingers brush the suckling mouth of the activator. Filaments in her glove reconfigure, anticipating contact. *Almost.*

Pike's black tendril snaps suddenly around her waist. Nikela gasps as the coils tighten, crushing her ribs. She would scream, but the attack has driven all the air from her lungs. The edges of her vision blur to gray, to red. The pain blinds her, erases all other thoughts.

Another glistening tendril slithers from the ruin of Pike's torso. It's smaller than the first, with a barbed end the color of dull bone.

Nikela's lungs burn from lack of oxygen. Her biotic suit attempts to compensate by injecting an emergency dose of OxGen8 into her bloodstream. It helps her stay conscious but does nothing for the pain. More ribs snap, dull explosions of agony.

A hissing sound gurgles from Pike's chest cavity. More words.

"Darlin', I'm gonna have to *make* you see things my way, I reckon." The barbed tendril bashes against her helmet. Once. Twice. The third time, there's a crack. Nikela nearly faints, but something keeps her awake.

You wanted to meet him, Nikela screams at herself. *And it's cost you everything.*

A third tendril snakes around her neck, crushing the seals of her helmet. The barb wriggles through the shattered collar, its dull tapping audible even through the roar of escaping air.

Nikela shudders, feels the warm talon scraping at her throat.

It's okay, kid. I got you. A comforting, familiar voice. Not Pike.

An explosion of light blinds her, and darkness finally comes.
And then Nikela feels herself falling, falling.

7.

Consciousness returns.

It surprises Nikela that she's not dead. Then it terrifies her. Her cheek rests naked against the spongy fungal soil of Crockett. The reek leaves ample space for agony. Her right side feels like it's on fire while her left aches with a cold like the vacuum of space. Roaring fills her ears. She gulps airlessly as the gale tears through her exposed ribs. Saints, Pike had cracked her *open*.

Her exosuit chirps constant alarms. It's the only thing keeping her alive. And only barely.

Pike is everywhere—bloody gobs of flesh and biotic rot raining from the sky. *Had he exploded again?* He coats her like a sizzling frost, firing her nerves and scrambling the haptic feedback from her suit. Saints of shit, he was colonizing *her*.

She grits her teeth, tasting blood. The Company didn't warn her how fast Pike would be. How deranged.

How *alien*.

She'd been too focused on the reunion, confident in their shared humanity despite the monstrous first life he'd led. She'd overridden her own concerns about the mission.

It didn't matter if she died. The Company would come back. She'd become the mission objective now. Half herself, half Pike. Something for the Company scientists to study. To dissect.

To weaponize.

Biotic scales blister up from her ruined flesh. He's knitting himself back together *on her*. She won't have the strength to stop him next time. With gut-wrenching certainty, she realizes she won't have the strength to stop herself either.

Poor Mai still does though.

Nikela claws herself across the slimy ground toward the fallen marine. The lights in Mai's chest flicker from green to amber. A high-pitched whine cuts through the roaring in her ears. The warp bomb, still trying to arm itself.

She'll help it help *her*.

Electric fire tears through her nerves, and explosions of agony leach color out of the world, but she plunges a finger into the activator, giving the sample required to arm it.

All she has to do is let go and the countdown starts.

Let the Company just fucking *try* to retrieve her. "C-Choi," she keys her comm, ignoring the dull cold beginning to spread up from her toes. "Abort mission. Clear OpZone."

The channel crackles with emptiness for long seconds before Choi responds. "Captain!"

Choi sounds closer somehow. The roaring in her head is not just in her head. The ground quakes with the force of thrust engines. Nikela smells it now, the burnt lightning aroma of a ship-mounted plasma cannon. The reason Pike's in a billion pieces.

From the corner of her eye, she sees three shapes emerge from the lowered ramp of *Convex*. Choi's in the lead, her sidearm up. A pair of suit-lights scrape over the grisly scene.

"Saints of shit," Choi gasps over the comm. "Help me, Lira."

One of the suited figures steps forward, a stimbulb in hand. Lira kneels by Nikela, her sapphire eyes gleaming. She frowns at Mai's body and the damage done to Nikela's exosuit.

Nikela waves off the offered pain meds. She can't lose consciousness, not with her finger in the detonator.

Lira doesn't understand and administers the drug anyway but freezes as she notices the bomb. "Saints of shit, Abreu," she breathes.

The meds bring a different sort of cold, washing through Nikela, a numbing relief. She jams her finger farther into the detonator lest her will slip.

"Warp bomb. Get out of here," she mumbles to Lira.

Choi's eyes are panicked. "Virgin's taint, Captain. Why didn't you tell us?"

"As soon as I let go," Nikela says, "point seven-five yield. The whole continent scraped clean. Should kill even . . . Pike."

Lira nods. In the thin lines of her lips, Nikela sees she understands.

Choi is still trying to save the mission, save her captain.

"Nikki," Choi stammers, "come on. We can't leave you here."

Nikela's able to grin. The pain meds help her feel more herself. "You can, Carin," she tells her engineer. "And you have to. I'm infected. You can't stuff my guts back inside."

The words are so ridiculous; Nikela almost laughs at herself. Then she feels the first slithering whispers of Pike's presence in her mind. Her body. Her laugh almost sounds like his.

"She's right," Lira says, backing away.

Does she sense what's happening?

"Damn you, Lira. You're not a sisterfucking medic," Choi snarls. Tears glimmer.

A third figure steps into Nikela's line of vision. Unsuited against the toxic planet.

Dad.

The one that raised us.

Abe's appearance fills her with a white-hot rage. Pike's influence fans the embers. He hates Abe Mistri for reasons Nikela is still too human to quite understand.

"Hello, Nikki," her dad says, leaning in. The pain etched into his face cruelly twists at Nikela's heart.

Goddamn bastard. You don't have any saint-shitting right to be here. You can't—

Abe Mistri lays his hand on her ruined side, and the relief is instant. A golden heat flows through her. For a moment, the deathly cold retreats. Her pressure on the warp bomb's detonator gets steadier.

"I haven't been much of a father," he says, "but I'm better than *him*."

Tears sting her eyes. *Goddamn you.* "You don't get to save me."

Her dad smiles. "Fair enough. But will you let me help you save your crew?" He looks meaningfully at Lira. Tears appear in the navigator's eyes as well.

"Oh gods. No, Abe," the synthetic says.

"I told you, Lira. I can't leave."

"But I just found you again."

A roaring fills Nikela's head as tendrils of light thread through her. She feels them holding back Pike's insistent presence. There's something else too, a curious hope kindled as her body begins to let go. Her dad has constructed a bulwark of starlight against the coming dark.

The mission has failed.

But finally, at long last, maybe Abe Mistri, her father, has not.

8.

The run out of Crockett is uneventful. Choi doesn't bother with a stealthy exit. There are no Colonial patrol vessels waiting for them in orbit. With Lira's help, *Convex* slips through the quantum mess again, though in truth the gradient storms subside as they near, almost as if the planet wants them to leave before the warp bomb detonates.

From a safe distance, Lira and the crew witness the implosion. A fury of spacetime scrubs a quarter of the planet clean, flattens it in dimensions normal sensors are inadequate to display. It hurts Lira's eyes to even look at the simulation. No ship will ever penetrate the resulting storm again.

Lira communes with *Convex*. The ship is silent on the fates of Abe Mistri, Durance Pike, and Nikela Abreu. No signals escape that stochastic storm, but Lira feels they are still alive somehow.

Convex knows the way through the open wounds of spacetime to the safety of the outer fringes of the system. Choi gives her uncharted coordinates for a second jump too. That destination is classified.

Lira doesn't like it, but she makes the calculations. She has no choice really. Her final duty performed, she leaves the bridge to Choi and the rest and heads to her quarters, aching with exhaustion like she's never known. In the corridors, *Convex* sings to her, despite the biotic shielding.

Sleep, Lira. Sleep.

She awakes in a flop sweat later in her bunk. She's still wearing the underlayer of her exosuit. It glows, pulsing with her heartbeat. She lurches to her feet and strips it off, her breath catching as the garment crumples to the deck.

Attached to the chest of the suit's haptic inner layer is a white, pearly sphere the size of her thumb. It pulses with a warm, restorative light—the same light Abe spread over his dying daughter.

She stares, remembering Abe's final embrace in the atrium and how her exosuit's power had fluctuated.

Saints of shit. What did you do, Abe?

Lira picks up the sphere and rolls it in her hand. Body temperature, slightly springy, and lightweight.

A spore, she thinks. *A seed.*

A ripple passes beneath the iridescent surface. The motion reminds Lira of Abe's smile somehow. Of their happy times together. She can't help but smile.

Abe came with me after all.

She wants to believe that, but that doesn't feel quite right.

Lira wants to go home, return to Oleander. To plant this seed there and see what grows. But Choi has another destination in mind and other masters to obey. Lira sees no future for herself wherever that is.

The comm chimes. "Second warp shunt in five minutes, Lira," Choi says. "You might want to strap in."

It almost sounds like acting-captain Carin Choi is pleading with her to do something.

Leave, says a voice that sounds like *Convex.*

Leave? she thinks. *How? Where would I go?*

Lira toys with the fittings on the hypersleep cuff, remembering the escape pods.

She slips back into her exosuit, carefully holding Abe's spore close against her chest. She reaches an escape pod just as the ship begins countdown for warp shunt.

Convex seems to be counting slowly. Or maybe time has slowed. Lira feels dizzy, like she did once on *Grass is Greener*, but her head is clear, her thoughts her own. The corridor lights turn blue as she enters the pod, the signal that most of the crew is going under soporific electrodes for the long jump. They won't notice she's gone until they awake at their destination.

She straps into the couch, relaxing. The pod comes alive around her. A fragment of the ship's consciousness reassures her. She activates the pod's own soporific electrodes, full of confidence and hope. The escape pod has an emergency warp beacon.

Someone will come along.

A jolt of acceleration and the pod sails free. She almost cheers, but Lira grows sleepy. She places Abe's pearl-spore back in her kit bag and sets it under her head, a pillow.

Lira begins to dream of Abe. Happy dreams this time.

PART 3: TEARS AMONG DIAMONDS

There shouldn't be an escape pod hanging in their flight path, yet there is.

Cam sees it before the rest of the crew does, a blip, a fragment of mystery in the void. A burning bit of life where there shouldn't even be dead rock.

"Onieogu," she warns, leaning over to hiss in the pilot's ear.

Onieogu starts awake, warning lights still burnishing his brassy face. Cam jabs a finger at him and then to the main holo. He yawns, his dark eyes full of confusion and annoyance.

"Prophet's taint, Cam, what is it?"

"A distress beacon."

Onieogu shakes his head, knuckling the sleep from his eyes. He's not just the pilot on *Tears Among Diamonds*—but the skipper too. Cam operates the sensors and the comms. Qae Carlisle is the engineer, though she's below-deck, asleep in her bunk. The tug steers itself in a long orbit around the massive blue-white Mehdi's Star, usually without much input from the crew.

That said, the AI autopilot aboard *Tears* is a little dumb. The biotic cores of a generation ago might have even handled the contract without any humans aboard, but no one was growing smart biotic cores anymore. Not since the Rot.

The Rot is why *Tears* is in this remote system. Decommissioned biotic core factories drop out of warp space at the edge of the system, and then Cam and her crew tow the massive stations into decaying orbits around Mehdi's Star. They're ancient facilities, no big loss really, rigged with outdated biotics—flawed designs susceptible to the Rot. Cam wonders sometimes what it would be like to go aboard, to hear the old engines sing.

She doesn't dream of breaking their contract with the Company in such a foolish and dangerous manner though. Besides the extreme risk, she couldn't talk to the cores the way synthetics from twenty or thirty years ago could. Cam is a newer class of synthetic, a better one. She's got fewer biotic nodes, and her core components are both sealed in the latest anti-Rot tech and sheathed with retro-nanites.

No one in the colonies wants another synthetic revolution like what happened on Silas's Crossing twenty years ago, so older biotics had been phased out.

"Transponder shows the pod belongs to a packet ship called *Convex Dissipation of Starlight*," she reports.

Onieogu shrugs. "Never heard of it."

Cam punches in a query to the AI but with the expected negative results. No record in the Company's logs, but their contract only allowed them access to the basic databases.

"We should wake Carlisle. We're required by contract to inform the crew of ships in distress."

"Uh, Qae's still asleep in my bunk. Last night—"

Cam cuts him off, uninterested in the latest escapades of her human crewmates. It's not that she begrudges their intimacy—as a synthetic, she's capable of the physical act. There's a certain amount of emotional contact required though, and while Cam has tried, she just finds there are other things more worth investing in. The contract, for one.

"Skipper. I've got biometric signs," she says, proving her point. "There's someone in the pod. *Alive.*"

Onieogu unstraps. He studies Cam's readings, brow furrowed.

"Hypersleep system shows green." He adds darkly, "That doesn't mean the occupant is alive."

Cam's smile is tight. She's already considered that. "Occupants. And I think they're synthetics."

The skipper's eyes go wide. "Saints of shit," he gasps.

Cam nods. "The pod's an old design. They might have been drifting out here for some time. Before the Rot."

Onieogu scratches the stubble on his chin. "And *we've* been out here four standard months, dragging those factories into Mehdi's Star. How are we just now spotting it?"

The skipper's question masks his true concerns. Pre-Rot synthetics, floating in a tiny husk of powered metal, just happening to cross their path in a volume of interplanetary space millions of cubic kilometers. There aren't many of them left, and Cam's never met one. She'd love to talk with these spacers, to learn what it was like for synthetics before fear of the Rot changed everything.

A little thrill passes through her as she realizes that the colonial law to rescue survivors in lifepods means she might get a chance after all. "Calibrating tractor array now, Skipper. I can have them aboard within the hour."

The skipper shakes his head, a little bead of sweat forming in the stubble of hair atop his brow. He checks some figures on his console.

"The next factory's due to drop from warp in two days, Cam, and we'll have to deviate course and burn a lot of extra fuel to catch that pod, even with the array."

Irritation prickles Cam's cheeks. Is the skipper suggesting they ignore the pod? "We're required by Colonial Protocol and contract to render aid," she insists. "You'd let someone die out there to make our schedule?"

Onieogu hangs his head, coloring with anger of his own.

"I'm not heartless, Cam," he sighs. "I'm just talking it out. Saints, we don't even know if those in that pod are still breathing. It's a lot of extra maneuvering, and our next fuel drop is more than six months out."

"Are you sure it's the fuel you're worried about?" She immediately regrets the accusation. Onieogu is her friend and business partner. He's never shown so much as a hint being a synthist.

Onieogu winces. "It *is* an older pod."

"Without a full biotic core, Skipper. Infection rates in older synthetic populations were never high. And before you bring up Silas's Crossing, remember that was engineered by those religious fanatics."

That was a local outbreak and quickly contained. Still, the event has fueled synthist attitudes for years. Regardless of colonial law, she knows what the Company will say if they head back out to the heliopause to send a clear signal: *leave them.*

She's not sure she can, contract or no. In truth, Cam's spent little time with other synthetics at all, another precaution against Rot. Would Onieogu deny her that chance?

"Skipper," she pleads, as much for herself as theoretical colonial law, "we can signal the Company after we've rescued them. You know it's the right thing to do."

Onieogu lets out a resigned sigh. "Alright, I'll go down and wake Qae. Get us a course and watch that fuel consumption."

Cam returns his tight smile and starts laying in a rendezvous plot. She ignores the knot in her abdomen, telling her the Company would never approve.

2.

From one dream to the next, the fog lifted. Sounds of buzzing like a hive of far-off insects. A hum that lingers on the edge of perception.

Lira is aware of warmth, a solid heat pressed against her side. She embraces it tightly. No, not it. *He.*

Another person.

Abe?

Too small. But he smells like Abe smells in her dreams.

Blinn. The other's name is Blinn, and he was in her dreams too.

Lira's eyes fly open to a bright fog of lights and blurry faces, concerned voices and droning machines. The distant thrum of a biotic core so remote and mechanical that she isn't sure that's what it is.

I'm on a ship, she thinks. *Rescue.*

One last tendril of fog lifts—the very solid hatch of her lifepod, her temporary sarcophagus. Lira gasps at the sudden, sharp tang of ship's air. The sleep 'trodes tear at her skin as she rips them away.

"Where?" she gasps to the ring of faces surrounding her.

When? Instinctively she knows she was in hypersleep for a long time. Her atrophied limbs ache, and her mouth tastes of dull metal.

"Easy there," says one of her rescuers, a young woman with dusky skin like

Abe's. *Nikela?* They'd reeled in her lifepod after all. But no, Captain Nikela Abreu had died on Crockett.

And Abe, who had died saving them all.

This newcomer had flatter features and a familiar kindness about her amber eyes that distinguished her from Nikela Abreu. There's a whisper of biotic processes about her too. A synthetic, but not a model Lira recognizes. The other spacers—a man with weathered brown skin and salt-and-pepper beard and a waspish woman, white and bald as a baby—fortunately bear no resemblance to the crew of *Convex Dissipation of Starlight.*

"Where," Lira croaked again with relief.

"*Tears Among Diamonds,*" the young woman spoke again. "You're safe."

Safe? Nothing is.

Lira remembers the feeling of Abe with her in the pod, in her long dreams, and she looks down. A child, maybe three years old, lay curled between her and the curved wall of the pod. Blinn. With olive skin and tawny hair. Blinn, who smells like Abe and tropical summers at their home on Oleander.

Blinn, who can't possibly be their child.

With a jolt, Lira recoils, leaping half out of the pod. The male spacer tries to grab her, but she crashes into the deck. Lira mouths other words, foul memories that curl on the tip of her tongue. Memories of Crockett and Abe and *godsdamn sisterfucking* Durance Pike.

"She's going into shock," the bald woman says, readying a hypobulb.

Lira shudders, remembering her long-ago addiction to stims. "No," she whimpers even as she longs for the old comfortable oblivion to release her from this confusion.

The bald one takes a step back, shoots a questioning glance at the male spacer. Lira pegs him as the captain. "Let her be," the captain says.

The compartment spins around her. It's a grubby little auxiliary bay with exposed bulkheads and flickering lights. Lira relaxes and takes a deep breath, drawing deep from all her years crewing ships like this one. Sort of like home. She almost smiles.

The synthetic spacer helps her to her feet. Lira's arm tingles, and she scowls a bit. The hum of the woman's biotic systems still seems too muted.

"Feel better?" the synth asks, her amber eyes glittering like holo-jewels that pierce Lira deep.

"Maybe."

"I'm Cam," the woman says. "*Tears Among Diamonds*'s comms op. What's your name?"

"Lira. So where are we?"

"Mehdi's Star. How'd you get out here?"

"I'm not sure. Last system I remember was Crockett."

Cam's expression darkens. In the long silence, Lira listens again for the faint pulse of Cam's biotic systems. They're muffled.

"Crockett's been dead for a long time, Lira," Onieogu says with a scowl. "No one's been there in at least twenty-five standards."

He exchanges worried glances with the rest of his crew. The bald woman looks especially nervous. Lira wonders how much is publicly known about what happened on Crockett. *Virgins' arsehole, I'm not even sure what really happened there.*

Aren't I?

"How's Blinn?" Lira peers, almost unwilling, into the pod. He's curled up around the life support leads, back against the side of the pod. He's a shade lighter than Abe's deep brown but otherwise looks so much like him it takes Lira's breath away. The line of his brow. The curl of his lips in an almost smile. Even the way his body rises and falls in the rhythms of sleep. Lira braces herself against the edge of the pod.

He looks like a five- or six-year-old human child.

Blinn's eyelids flutter, and the timber of his breathing changes. His tiny hands clench into fists. A six-year-old child unaged after a twenty-five-year journey. The hum of his biotics is nothing like what Lira's heard before, high and bright.

Cam leans in next to Lira, her expression darkening. There's a question in her amber eyes, burning hot as a star.

"He's synthetic too," Lira admits, though she has at least as many questions about that as Cam does. Abe's voice haunted her dreams all the way from Crockett, reminding her of his strange gift.

"How?" Onieogu almost shouts the question.

Lira flinches away from the big man and answers Cam instead. "An experiment," she says, truth enough for now. "The last ship I crewed on was likely extralegal."

As another synthetic, Cam might be a potential ally, but Lira can't trust her with what she knows, what she suspects, just yet.

"*Child* synthetics." Cam hisses her disapproval.

Ethical issues surrounding synthetic life had been settled by colonial law for decades, and there were strict laws about which sort of synthetics were grown and which were not. The true masters of *Convex* were likely the sort who'd ignore such laws. Let them shoulder blame until Lira knows more about her situation.

Lira holds up a placating hand. "Why do you think I fled *Convex*? I didn't want to be a part of their mission."

Cam sets her jaw, displeased, but she seems to be convinced by Lira's partial truths.

"Okay, sure, but Mehdi's Star?" Carlisle blurts out. Onieogu nods, obviously skeptical.

Lira shrugs.

"I'm not sure. Something to do with the ship's drive malfunctioning. We escaped in the pod as the ship was jumping out, and I—*we*—got caught on the edge of the warp bubble."

"Mehdi's Star," Onieogu repeats, crossing his arms.

"Maybe *Convex* warped here and left before they realized I was gone," she says. "Like I said, the ship had big secrets. What about this ship? What kind of secrets are you keeping? Why are *you* at a shit-system like this?"

Cam glances at her captain, and he nods. "*Tears Among Diamonds* is just a Company tug. We're flinging decommissioned biotics factories into the star."

Lira starts with a thrill of panic. The sisterfucking Company. Of course. Mehdi's Star is a long way to go to dispose of garbage, but the Company did a lot of things the hard way.

"The Rot," Cam explains, anticipating Lira's question.

The answer confuses Lira for moment until she recalls her last planetfall. "Like what happened on Crockett?"

Cam waggles her head. "From everywhere. It hit Crockett hard, but that wasn't the only place. Old-type biotic cores were most susceptible, so they stopped growing them. They found problems with the factories too. So we get paid to make sure they burn up."

Lira examines the tug crew's faces. They're all worried she's infected—and Blinn too. She swallows a sudden surge of panic and asks with a level voice. "So are you going to do the same to us?"

Cam looks away, embarrassed, and then back with a slightly irritated expression. "Of course not. You scanned clean, or we wouldn't have brought you aboard."

Carlisle steps forward, wearing a dubious expression. "Those religious freaks on Silas's Crossing scanned clean too. We all know how that ended up."

Lira turns cold.

"That's why they designed models like me," Cam explains. "We're immune. They stopped growing the cores the old way too. The interface pathways are different. Less intimate. Warp trips take longer, sure, but the Rot's no longer an issue."

A sequence of alarms blast from the bay's comm panel. Onieogu checks his wrist comp. "That'll be our next tow, dropping out of warp. Factory 421B. Cam, why don't you get our passengers settled in. Qae, I need you on the bridge."

The two-human crew hurry out of the bay, leaving Lira alone with Cam.

When the humans have gone, Cam makes a suggestion. "I think we should try and wake Blinn," she says.

Lira reads the conflict in her determined expression. She must sense Lira's reticence too. The dreams had been easy. Actually talking to him—what if he sounds too much like Abe? In a dream, she'd played with Blinn in the surf of a golden Oleander beach. The memory of that endless afternoon dulls around the edges. Not real. Another twist of emotion knots her—fear, not anger. The Oleander beach is a lie. Abe had given her an unasked-for child to raise, but she'd taken him willingly from Crockett all the same.

Her pod had one emergency jump, and somehow, they'd crossed nearly a light-year to arrive at the even more remote Mehdi's Star. Fear again as she ponders what certainly must not be random chance. Had she calculated this jump in her sleep?

If so, then by whose design?

Not hers. The question of her autonomy had been settled long before. *Highline* was a lifetime ago. *Grass is Greener*. Crockett. Pike. The Rot had never infected her. Had Abe planted the destination in her head?

She clenches her fists. The old Abe wouldn't.

Lira toys with the life support controls. Toggle a few switches and tug on a few wires and Blinn would wake on his own. The other synthetic, Cam, watches with suspicion. Perhaps she might build some trust between her and Cam.

"I talk to Blinn sometimes. In my dreams," she admits to Cam.

There's a hooded look in Cam's eyes, a mixture of jealousy and fear perhaps. She pats Lira on the arm awkwardly. The younger synthetic may have advanced containment and a diminished interface, but for a brief moment, Lira feels a connection. Maybe Cam feels it too.

"Skipper plans to send a message to the Company after the rendezvous. Required by our contract," Cam's voice carries a hint of warning. She's sharing a secret too. "If we're going to hear his story, it better be now."

Lira nods. News that Lira has surfaced after Crockett will likely bring the Company running. Given Blinn's nature, everyone on *Tears* was in danger too. This is Lira's last chance to hear what Abe was trying to say all those years ago on Crockett.

"Alright. Let's do it," Lira says.

3.

Cam eyes Lira as she leans into the lifepod and toggles the wake sequence. A series of soft chimes sounds as the pod's life support disengages. Cam's apprehension flares. She'd convinced Onieogu to allow this, but a strange foreboding takes hold, like she's jammed a throttle wide open and is thrusting on a collision course.

"Blinn," Lira says softly. She takes his wrist, feeling for his pulse.

"Is he waking?" Cam asks.

Lira nods.

Cam's apprehension deepens. What sort of being is a top-secret synthetic child? Certainly not a naive one. Whoever designed him must have had a reason. *Convex* was probably owned by the Company—no one else had the kinds of funds necessary for high-end synthetic design.

They'd likely be eager to get Blinn—and even Lira—back. Cam could probably even expect a bonus for returning Company assets. In the meantime, she's got a chance to talk to a pair of advanced pre-Rot synthetics, to hear firsthand what it was like to live without inherently designed limitations.

Blinn stirs, eyes fluttering, limbs twitching. Lira holds her chin in her hand.

Cam detects a tremor. She suppresses a mirror response in herself and monitors the umbilical in the equipment bay. Life signs stable. Power nominal.

A shrill alarm erupts from the pod's systems. Blinn heaves a shuddering gasp and starts to scream. His eyes dart open, orbs of silver that stare at everything, stare at nothing. He strains against his restraints, pulling them taut. His screams transform to bestial howls. Lira steps back, shaking. A moan escapes her lips.

Something wrenches deep in Cam as Blinn attempts to free himself. Not a maternal instinct, no, but mirror longing to escape the constraints her designs have placed on her. For an instant, she thinks she understands Blinn. And Lira too.

The child's heart rate spikes and then drops to almost nothing. Lira reaches for him with unheard words. Blinn calms for only an instant before another scream tears out like oxygen blasting out of an airlock.

His empty eyes find Cam's for a moment. Something electric surges through her, and she can almost hear words. Words that sound like—

Help me, Cam.

Saints of shit. Cam lurches forward, slapping at the life support switches and plunging Blinn back into an induced coma. It takes several seconds for the 'trodes to take hold.

Outwardly, Blinn's screams trail to whimpers, to nothing. His breathing becomes deep again.

"What in the Virgin's arsehole was that?" Cam turns to Lira. Tears run from her sapphire eyes. She shakes, eyes are full of terror.

"Did you feel it?" Lira says.

Cam narrows her eyes. No, no. She doesn't have the pathways. She felt nothing, but maybe she heard something.

"Feel what?" She dares Lira to name it. Make it real.

Lira holds her finger in the air, tracing a line between her and Blinn. Between Cam and the bulkhead. The lights on the umbilical readout are a scramble of color. It had nearly overloaded seconds before. "He made a connection. With *Tears Among Diamonds.*" Lira whispers, eyes wide. "Maybe farther out too."

Cam shakes her head. Does she mean Factory 421B too? That's impossible. Biotic connections, let alone long-range communications, require special interfaces. Interfaces Tears doesn't have.

"The umbilical," Lira insists.

"That system is fully mechanical," Cam protests. Still, her hand moves involuntarily toward the comm panel to alert Onieogu.

She hesitates. Blinn had spoken to *her*. That wasn't supposed to be possible either. She doesn't have the proper pathways. Biotic-somatic feedback does sometimes occur, but Cam's only read about it in Company manuals. Could it be a sign of Rot, a symptom? Maybe Onieogu was right. They shouldn't have taken these pre-Rot synthetics aboard.

Lira stands rigid, fists clenched. She's shaking, paler than usual.

"Lira, I think we'd better get you to the infirmary."

Steel comes into the older synthetic's eyes. "No. Not the *ship*."

Cam cocks her head. What the hell is Lira babbling about? Is she still talking to Blinn? She takes Lira by the shoulder. The woman rips out of her arms, sapphire eyes blazing.

Blinn's screams echo in her ears like some sort of insane melody. Cam holds her hands to her head, realizing she's letting down her guard. She's strong like all synthetics, yes, but she isn't sure of Lira's capabilities. As a refugee from a secretive operation, she could be a combat model.

Lira's tension suddenly drains, and she collapses like a severed hydraulic line. Blinn's song stops too. Cam crouches, both irritated and relieved she can't hear him anymore.

"Infirmary. Yes. For the best," Lira says, as groggy as if she'd just awoken from hypersleep.

Lira is pliant, almost eager, as Cam guides her out of the engineering bay and aft toward the infirmary. Only after they pass through the second pressure hatch, safely away from Blinn, does Cam dare speak to Lira.

"What did Blinn say to you?" she demands as they rest against a bulkhead.

Lira's expression clears. "On *Grass is Greener*, our problems started as white noise on the comms as biotic matter sung to biotic matter. On Crockett, it was a deafening chorus. What we just heard was just a single note but even more potent. I think we're compromised. I think *everything's* compromised."

Cam's breath catches in her throat. Her gut feels cold. What the hell does Lira mean by *everything*?

Not fucking *Tears*. The core is too heavily shielded. No one can communicate with it unless they're plugged into one of the two special consoles aboard.

Cam tells Lira as much.

Lira shrugs. "He doesn't have the limits *other* synthetics do."

Cam reddens as Lira's unintentional barb stabs deep. Fear burns away any personal jealousy. Onieogu and Carlisle must be alerted that the ship might be infected. But first, the infirmary. Lira strapped in, asleep and not talking nonsense to anyone. The infirmary door hisses open.

"Please lie down, Lira," Cam says, trying to keep her voice steady as she hooks the other woman to the sleep 'trodes. She'd insisted on this rescue. She couldn't let them die out here. But it's her fault they woke them up before contacting the Company. She fucked up.

Lira lies obediently back and attaches one 'trode herself. "Maybe I can reach him in our dreams. Make him let go of *Tears*. Wake me when it's safe."

"Sure," Cam says. Her face is leaden. Lira might never wake up. Not on the tug anyway. Onieogu might space her and Blinn both after this. Or more likely, he'd turn them over to the Company without a qualm.

What would the Company do with *her*, a synthetic willing to put the ship in so much danger? Might they question her loyalties? Should they? She shudders.

Will the captain?

"There's more out there," Lira mumbles as the soporific electrodes take hold. Her eyelids drift, but her lips keep moving with whispers.

A bright shock of fear streaks through Cam. "What the hell, Lira? More what?"

But Lira falls asleep. As her breathing deepens, her right hand starts to twitch.

The comm buzzes, and Onieogu's voice, gritty with anger, crackles through.

"We just read a power surge on the bridge, Cam. You wanna tell me what the hell just happened?"

Cam collapses onto the acceleration couch across from where Lira sleeps. Somehow, *I may have just fucked us all,* doesn't seem like the right response.

"We tried to wake Blinn, but there's something wrong with him."

Onieogu's exasperated sigh crackles out of the comm. "I need more than that, Cam. We're coming up on the rendezvous."

"The kid's asleep again. And I just put Lira under." *Onieogu is worried.*

"That doesn't sound good. Tell me what actually happened."

Cam winces at the accusation implicit in the captain's words. "Blame me. Put it on my record."

There's a long silence over the comm, broken only by the background hum of the ship's systems. "Get your ass up to the bridge, Cam."

"Roger, sir."

Cam stands in the med bay for a moment, thinking.

She opens a panel on the medical locker, parts the rudimentary emergency exosuits hanging inside. On a shelf behind them is a Nonter-75 neurostunner. Regulations stipulate the weapons to be stored in a secure locker or ship's armory, but this far out from the colonies, Onieogu had packed a little extra.

"We're pushing a lot of valuable tech into Medhi's Star," he'd reminded her and Qae as he handed out the weapons. "If anyone knew we were out here without escort, they might be tempted. I'd rather be prepared, wouldn't you?"

Cam had another one of the snub-nosed pistols stashed in her quarters and a buzz-knife hidden in her boot. They'd never so much as commed a flicker of a pirate vessel, but Cam felt better with the weapons close by.

They could look after the Company's interests better if they looked after themselves, right?

She studies Lira's sleeping face, the curve of her brow. Eyelids twitching with hypersleep. *Does she dream about the ship? About Blinn?* Cam feels another flash of jealousy that Lira, antiquated as she is, can still feel the faint thrums of *her* sisterfucking ship. Can feel *anything* biotic.

Cam hooks the stunner to her belt and steps out into the corridor. She seals the infirmary hatch behind her with her personal code. Only she gets in.

She dismisses the thought and concentrates instead on the upcoming job. Lira and Blinn are a complication for the Company to handle. The sooner they get 421B into is final orbit, the sooner they get back on schedule.

4.

Twelve hours later, *Tears Among Diamonds* burns hard on final approach to Factory 421B, hull yokes extended. Even with the looming superstructure of the factory-ship finally filling the viewport, Onieogu still grumbles about schedules and their castaways.

"How are the scans?" he asks Cam. He doesn't look at her when he asks. She notices he can't quite meet her eye. It's still her fault they brought the pair aboard. She feels a flicker of anger. She had only been following protocol.

Still, Cam sighs with relief and flicks the latest data to the main holo for the skipper to study. A report every hour on the hour. As before, no sign of any contagion in the ship's systems. No sign of the Rot.

Cam's actually been scanning every fifteen minutes, pinging the biotic core of *Tears* for any anomalies. Lira babbled that Blinn had already infected everything, but Cam can't find a single trace of troubling data to backup that fear. She's even risked a quick interface with the core. Everything was nominal. Green lights all the way.

If only I could interface more completely, she thinks with only a trace of jealousy. Probably for the best though. She's safe. The ship's safe. Lira's paranoia is understandable but merely amplified by being in hibernation for so long.

"All scans negative," she tells Onieogu. The skipper's relief is palpable as he swigs from his tea.

Carlisle sighs at her station. She's run a dozen checks on the life support system for every one of Cam's.

"No spikes in biotic growth," she reports. "Oxygen and humidity levels are pretty much spot on."

The Rot had a way of gulping carbon dioxide, expelling an excess of oxygen and other volatile gases—not good in a pressurized environment like a ship.

Onieogu's face clouds, and a surge of apprehension rises in Cam.

"What?"

Onieogu finally looks her in the eyes, his troubled expression deepening.

"It's time to transmit a report to the Company, Cam."

Cam frowns. It's as much a part of protocol and contract as the requirement to pick up survivors, yet she's anxious about how they'll respond.

"It will probably take a few days to hear back," Onieogu replies, his demeanor softening. "By that time, we'll have finished the tow on 421B. It'll give us all time to talk through what we're going to say."

"Skipper, what's the rush? We could transmit after we drop off the factory." That would be an extra few days to talk to Lira. Find out more about Blinn. Maybe they could even try to wake him again—disconnected from the pod of course.

Carlisle shoots the skipper a worried look. Cam chews her lip, annoyed at all the loaded glances her crewmates are exchanging.

"C'mon, Cam. We've played enough roulette here," Carlisle says. "They might be clean, but there'll be penalties for the delay in reporting. Our margins are thin enough out here."

"'Clean', Carlisle?" Cam fights an urge to deck the engineer. She's sounding like a synthist.

"Enough!" Onieogu shouts, face blotchy with sudden anger.

"Saints of shit, Cam. Don't paint us secret synthists. We've been tight for a long time. You know that's not us. I'm just looking after my ship. And *all* my crew."

Maybe that's so, but Cam can take a hint. She unstraps herself from her console and turns for the exit.

"Where are you going?" Onieogu demands.

"I'm going to run the next few scans from engineering," she says. A little space will help her cool down. She tries to pretend her human crewmates don't exchange another worried look as she goes.

Onieogu transmits their report to the board of supervisors. The next four hours pass in brisk efficiency. The crew of *Tears* does its job. They dock with 421B, adjust course, and burn for Mehdi's Star. Its blue-white disk grows in the holoport, plots of its predicted solar prominences—prime insertion points for the doomed factory-ship—flickering in the main display. Onieogu busies himself with charting optimal release projections. In stony silence, Cam, returned from engineering, feeds him numbers collated from the ship's core—safe paths through the worst of the quantum shear emanating deep from the photosphere.

More hours tick by, and Mehdi's Star gets larger in the viewport. To Cam's relief, their message to the Company remains unanswered even as they approach the insertion point.

From her earliest days, the Company that raised her taught her that some natural-borns are uneasy around synthetics. It had always been so, even before that uprising on Silas's Crossing.

Gaspar Onieogu had never shown a gram of synthist prejudice, but his strange behavior over the last few hours makes Cam feel like maybe she'd never known her skipper and engineer at all. Maybe she hasn't. Despite their initial intimacy, Cam has remained somewhat aloof as professionally required.

She considers requesting a transfer after this contract is up. She might even go for a skipper rating herself. She's more than qualified to handle a tug, and there are plenty of synthetic captains.

Onieogu gives strict orders not to wake Lira or Blinn. Running her scans, Cam paces the ship, pausing to look in on Lira in the infirmary and Blinn in his pod. Their eyelids twitch in dreaming sleep. She can't talk to them. Are they talking to each other? Cam burns to know.

Lira's a link to the old days—days Cam didn't live through but that have been programmed into her core as thoroughly as any childhood nightmare. Three colony worlds overrun by the Rot. At least a hundred ships. Five million dead, synthetics and organics alike.

And somehow Lira—and Blinn—had survived all of that. Cam had to know how. Maybe it was something in her design. Something in the old navigation pathways that Cam's generation lacked. Maybe it was even something Lira could teach her.

If she could only talk to her again before the Company arrived.

They finally release 421B as the ship's night approaches, and the factory begins its long descent down into the final embrace of the blue giant star at maximal acceleration. It will burn up long before gravity crushes it, of course. On the bridge, a chill silence reigns. Carlisle makes a play at being peacemaker.

"All systems green," she reports. "No trace of contamination." Her relieved smile isn't forced, and Cam finally lets some of her anger go. She takes a breath, turns to Onieogu.

It's only a momentary peace. Carlisle's brow furrows as lights flicker across a different engineering panel.

"That's odd," she says throwing a toggle. Her frown deepens. "The umbilical in bay two is dropping power. Wait, no. It's completely shut down."

"The lifepod?" Onieogu's voice rises with concern.

"Virgin's arsehole, Skipper," she shouts. "It's disconnected. Ship, show me engineering two."

Carlisle switches to a holo feed, and it goes dark.

"Carlisle," Onieogu says, glancing at Cam.

She's already unstrapping from her couch, stunner close at hand. The data from the infirmary shows Lira, sleeping. There's only one other person aboard who could have disconnected that power umbilical.

An alarm blares from Onieogu's station.

PRESSURE LOSS. DECK TWO.

"Saints of shit!" Carlisle shouts, though Cam's hardly surprised.

"Blinn," Onieogu darkens.

"But he was asleep right up until we lost power," she says, heading to check it out.

Cam pauses at the hatch at Carlisle's strangled cry. The engineer jabs a finger at the holo display. A streak of light stabs away from *Tears Among Diamonds*, bending in a long arc back toward Factory 421B.

Saints of shit indeed.

"Is that the lifepod?" Cam asks.

Carlisle nods furiously, sweat beading up on her brow.

"Full burn on course for the factory-ship. Reading one life sign aboard."

"It's that fucking kid," Onieogu curses.

On the holo, the pod fires thrusters and vectors on a close approach to the factory. Onieogu shakes his head.

"What's he doing? That factory will enter the photosphere in less than four hours. He'll be vaporized along with . . . everything else over there."

Cam scowls. What *else* is over there?

"How the hell are we going to explain this?" Onieogu grumbles. "We already accrued 44K in late penalties. Add a Rot-infected factory, vaporized or not, and we'll be paying off contract violations for the rest of our saints-shitting lives."

He's right. The Company will tear their ship—their *lives*—apart, looking for signs of Rot and asking hard questions about their professional judgment. They'll be blacklisted from every guild and franchise operation for the rest of their days.

That's before they'll inquire how a child—a synthetic child somehow mixed up in the Crockett incident—came to be aboard *Tears* and how this child, while in hypersleep, managed to open engineering's airlock and fly his lifepod four hundred thousand kilometers toward the factory.

Despite that dire outcome though, Cam's thoughts keep returning to what the skipper had said moments before. *What else is in the factory?* Whatever it is must matter to Blinn, and they can't trust him alone over there. Cam is overtaken with a sudden need to know too.

"Captain, we've got to go after him," Cam says. "Whatever he's up to over there can't be good."

"Another contract violation," Onieogu swears, but his expression is resigned. "Okay. Carlisle and I will—"

"Let *me* go, sir."

Onieogu raises an eyebrow, already shaking his head no. Cam doesn't give him a chance to say it. Now's her chance.

"Let me take Lira along."

Onieogu throws up his hands, incensed. And something else. Afraid?

"Absolutely not, Cam. It's too big a risk, putting them together again."

Cam nods. He's right, but he's also hiding something—from her, his second in command. *Is it because she's a synthetic? Is there something about them, about her, the skipper's hoping to conceal?* Her suggestion is sound otherwise. Lira's the one with history with Blinn. She's the only one who'll be able to cut through his weird static, calm him down, and bring him back.

She reminds Onieogu of that. The captain shakes his capsule of tea, looking at it like he wants to crawl inside. A strange resignation crosses his face.

Prophet's taint, Cam," he sighs, "I know I can't fucking stop you from going." He glances at her and at Carlisle. "But I want you to know I tried."

Something in the look between her crewmates makes Cam even more uneasy. Whatever Onieogu knows, Carlisle knows it too. Cam suddenly feels the weight of the stunner clipped to her belt.

"Thanks, Skipper. You can count on me."

As Cam exits the bridge though, she wonders if *she* can count on Onieogu.

5.

Blinn has vanished from her dreams. Lira walks the twilit beaches of Oleander alone, wading ankle deep in the warm surf. She studies the cliffside for the path that leads back to her house. Abe's house. The succulents with the little purple buds have grown wild though, and rakeweed has carpeted the dunes. The path is gone.

If it was ever there.

Somewhere up on those cliffs—she senses that's where Blinn has gone. Where maybe Abe awaits too. Once, these beaches were familiar to her; now, she's hopelessly lost.

"Lira," a voice behind her. Cam, the synthetic from *Tears Among Diamonds*.

She turns to greet the other woman. Cam looks upset, trembling with a mixture of fear and anger. The Oleander twilight vanishes in the cold lights of the infirmary. She blinks away hypersleep, aboard *Tears* once again. The loss of Blinn remains an ache though.

"He's gone," she mumbles to Cam.

Cam nods. "I need your help to get him back."

Lira sits up, removing the sleep cuff. Cam holds out a spare set of white coveralls. Lira notices the ugly muzzle of a high-powered stunner clipped to Cam's belt too. Looks like she's going with Cam whether she wants to or not. Coercion isn't necessary.

"That isn't for you," Cam says, seeing her wince. The troubled look in her amber eyes deepens.

"For Blinn?"

"Maybe," she admits. "I don't know what he wants."

Cam's admission is really a question. Lira doesn't know either.

"I dreamed he was gone."

"Saints of shit, Lira. He blew the airlock in engineering somehow. Took your lifepod straight to the factory-ship. What is he up to?"

Lira sighs, wishing she had an answer for Cam. She climbs out of the infirmary bed and slips into the white coveralls Cam offers. Her legs wobble. She just wants to go back to sleep.

"What's really in the factories?" she asks.

Cam's lips press into a tight line.

She wants to trust me but doesn't know if she can.

Lira can't blame her.

"As far as I know, biotic cores, decommissioned. Old type, susceptible to Rot but not actually infected."

"You don't think that's all though."

Cam looks away, pretends to study Lira's med monitor.

"Skipper knows more, but I guess I don't have the clearance."

Cam's words are heavy with bitterness.

Lira, still dizzy, steadies herself against the bed. Prophet's arsehole. At the very least, she guesses Blinn might try to engage the biotic cores that run the factory and its warp drives. Cam confirms her fears.

"At the height of the epidemic, there was a rash of ships just warping away, Lira. All on their own, no navigators required. None of them came back."

"You believe that's what Blinn wants? To warp away?"

Lira shudders. It's a scenario akin to her old nightmares after *Highline*. On the one hand, if Blinn warped away, she'd be rid of him. On the other, he's her last link to Abe.

"We can't let him," Cam says. "That's why I need you."

The desperate look in Cam's eyes tells Lira there's something more, but she leaves it for now, more worried about Blinn. He had been an *it* once and had seemed at the time something pure, a pearl made of the best of Abe Mistri. A distillation of the part of him that still loved her. Blinn is not what she'd expected from that gift.

Now, the child's single-minded actions seemed more and more to her like another person's, during the last hours of *Grass is Greener*.

Durance Pike.

Nikela Abreu's warp bomb obliterated an entire continent on Crockett along with the reborn cultist Pike—as well as that final manifestation of Abe. Was it possible both still lived within the strange biotic ties that seemed to thread the universe after contact with that sinister comet?

Once more, she wonders—is she weaving these threads or being woven by them? She scowls as Cam hurries her down a corridor to another airlock. Beyond the hatch, a launch waits in its U-shaped cradle. The delicate craft seems incongruous with the tug's otherwise functional design.

Lira hears the distant hum of the tug's biotic core as it angles to a launch vector.

"We're in position," Onieogu says over the comms. "Bring him back. And yourself too, Cam. We *need* you."

Cam punches in a code to the exosuit alcove. Lira's unsettled by the way Onieogu stressed the word *need*. The empty suits swing like ghosts in their alcove. Cam pulls one from its hook and begins to shrug it on.

"Roger, Captain. We'll be in touch," she says in monotone. Cam doesn't trust the skipper, Lira realizes.

Lira loosens the seals on her exosuit. The haptic fibers aren't as responsive as the suits she remembers from before. *Another victim of the colonies' fear of biotics,* she supposes.

"What is he, really?" Cam peers at Lira with suspicion as she slides into her own suit. At first, she thinks she's talking about the skipper again. She realizes Cam means Blinn.

"I don't know," Lira says truthfully. She slips her feet into her boots. The haptic fabric conforms around her legs, stiffening in a protective seal as it comes online. A sudden sadness mantles over her as the suit wraps her in its embrace.

They strap into the cramped launch, and in moments, they are hurtling across the void toward Factory 421B.

Saints of shit, Abe. We never wanted children.

Whatever version of Abe manifested on Crockett had changed his mind about that. Changed *their* plan. An evil thought threads it way through her mind like a touch of Rot. *What if it hadn't been Abe on Crockett after all? What if that whole mess had been a ploy by the one who'd started it all?*

Durance Pike.

Could he be reaching across the grave—twice now—to inflict his malevolent conviction on the colonies? On her? Saints of shit, he's ruined her life far too many times for her to let him do it again.

"Any more weapons on board?" she asks Cam, trying not to sound desperate herself.

"Just the one, I'm afraid," she says with an uncertain look, patting her stunner.

Lira frowns. Fine. She can murder Pike with her bare hands if he's on that factory-ship.

All too soon, they dock with Factory 421B.

The airlock doors open, and a gust of factory air whooshes past. A chime in Lira's helmet indicates it's breathable, but oxygen levels are climbing. Rot. Beyond the airlock, a dark, low corridor plunges into the heart of tower three. Cam shines a suit light down the passageway. Inert biotic machinery glints in sheens of blue and gold. Thready black-and-yellow curtains of biotic matter hang from the low ceilings, swaying like ghosts in the ventilation drafts. Lira's pulse quickens.

Maybe Pike *is* here.

Cam scans the hanging Rot with her suit's sensor suite, mumbling too low for Lira to hear. She steps carefully around a protrusion of Rot jutting from a life-support stanchion.

"Virgin's arsehole, is this what Crockett was like?"

Lira nods. "Worse, if you can believe it." She wishes she had a warp bomb on her.

"We're in tower three. Blinn docked at tower one, but there's a connecting bridge two levels up." Cam points to a holo map, emitting from her helmet, and stares at Lira intently.

"Unless you think he went elsewhere?"

Lira shakes her head.

"I can't sense him if that's what you're asking. We're not connected in that way."

"Too bad," Cam says with a grin. "That would have been too easy."

Lira returns a faint smile. She knows Blinn is aboard, but he isn't a sensor blip she can chart. She calls up Cam's schematic in her suit's own display. An array of amber lines assembles itself before her eyes.

"The control hub is definitely in tower one," she says. "It's positioned right above the main growth chamb—wait."

She feels a chill, even in the warm embrace of her exosuit. This data can't be right.

"What?" Cam asks, trembling.

"Look at this growth chamber." With a flick of her eyes, Lira slides the holo to Cam's suit display. She highlights the growth capsules. They're about three meters long each and arranged in tight rows of five by five, radiating off a central hub like an Oleander sea star.

"That's an odd configuration for growing biotic cores," Cam agrees. "I mean, those old generation cores were at least twenty meters across. Why divide the growth capsules like that?"

Lira starts sweating in her suit. She sees the answer to Cam's question written in the holo schematic as clearly as if she's looking at it with her own eyes. With shaking fingers, she adjusts the display from her wrist comp, switching to tower three and the factory levels below the deck at their feet.

"At least five more identical chambers in tower three," Lira says, shaking her head. How the hell could they get down there? Cam looks around at the myriad forms of biotic growth, a mix of horror and fascination on her face.

"How long have you served on *Tears*, Cam?" Lira asks. She suspects the other woman is in for a terrible shock.

"What do you mean?" Cam raises an eyebrow.

"Do you trust Carlisle and Onieogu?"

Cam frowns.

"They've been my friends and crewmates for almost ten years. Of course." Her declaration sounds a lot more like a question though.

"Have you slept with either of them?"

Cam shrugs.

"A little, but I didn't find the experience fulfilling. How does that matter?"

"Ah," Lira says. Sex isn't for everyone, of course, but is this a quirk of Cam's personality or some part of these new model synthetics that prevents them from the same sort of attachments to their human crew that Lira enjoyed? Enjoys.

She weighs how much to tell Cam, realizing this might be their last chance to talk before whatever comes next. Someone's got to know the whole sorry story, and she might as well tell Cam while they look for a way below.

"I don't understand how, but Blinn's existence is bound to a man who meant a great deal to me. My best friend. My lover. Abraham Mistri. He was the engineer on my old ship," Lira says. She begins to scan the bulkheads around them, looking for an access hatch or ladderwell. The thought of what might be below their feet tears at her like a riptide.

"The secretive one? *Convex*?" Cam asks.

"No, *Grass is Greener*. It was a passenger tug, ran the Silas's Crossing and Crockett route. Until we dropped out of warp in the wrong place. Found ourselves in the orbit of a fucked-up comet."

Cam laughs without humor.

"Full of Rot, I'm guessing."

"Good guess."

"What happened?"

The scanner beeps, and Lira kicks aside a clump of lumpy, hexagonal tubules. They tear apart like old fabric, spreading greenish clouds into the air. Beneath them gleams the sturdy handle of a ladderwell hatch.

"It's a long story, but we lost the ship. Lost each other. Abe died, but I saw him again on Crockett years later on the *Convex* mission. He helped some of us survive that disaster. And he gave me Blinn. Only, at the time, Blinn was some kind of seed, I guess."

Lira yanks open the hatch, sending more clouds of friable biotic matter in billows around them. Cam takes a step back.

"You're sounding warp-loopy, Lira," Cam says. She looks scared.

"It happened whether you want to believe me or not, Cam."

She peers down into the dark ladderwell, relieved to see that the sealed hatches meant it was free from Rot.

"Is it safe?" Cam asks, shining her light down the dusty crawlspace.

"Saints of shit, nothing's safe here," Lira says, "but if these chambers are what I think they are, then we'll know for sure why Blinn lead us here."

Cam gives her a quizzical look.

"Just follow me," Lira says, fighting another swell of panic.

Lira enters the well and descends to the next deck. A few scattered curtains of biotic matter hang across hatchways, but the whole level seems mostly untouched by the Rot that disfigures the deck above. Cam follows her down with only some hesitation. The worry is plain enough on her face though. She's thinking about the intimacy she lacked with her crew, still fears what they concealed from her.

Cam's amber eyes dart anxiously up and down the corridor as she exits the ladderwell.

The main hatch to the growth chamber is a short jog across the lightly contaminated deck. It opens at Lira's touch.

Beyond, the biotic growth chamber is cavernous, and its depths are lost to thick shadows—in contrast to the rest of the deck, boiling with Rot. It's a copy of the chamber they identified in tower one's schematics with at least four hubs of growth capsules, hints of many more glinting in the deeper dark. Threaded through them all are vast, tree-like structures of living rot, their trunks ribbed and lined with pulsing clusters of an oozing blue-green medium.

"Saints of sisterfucking shit," Cam gasps beside her. She goes rigid, staring hard at the impossibility of the factory floor.

Lira fights an urge to take the woman's hand. To comfort her, to hold onto something *real*, to deny what they both are seeing.

One hundred capsules arrayed in the banks immediately in front of them, probably five times as many filling the rest of the vast chamber. Each capsule is three meters long and filled with a milky blue-green biotic fluid. Nutrients. Growth medium—the same stuff leaking from the tree-like structures. The capsules' controls indicate minimal power, enough to keep the contents inside minimally viable.

Inside each of those capsules is a synthetic, curled in a fetal ball. Asleep, eyes fluttering in deep dream. Lira's gaze is frozen on the one nearest to her. It's a woman, floating in a repose from which she'll likely never awaken.

She's younger, still bald, and while her skin is shaded in a darker hue, there's no mistaking the familiarity.

She has Lira's face.

6.

Cam stares at the endless rows of umbilical pods, speechless. The inert synthetics hang stillborn in the soft blue-green light. Save for the distant background hum of auxiliary power, the cavernous chamber is silent. Yet Cam imagines she can almost hear a chorus of pleading whispers from the suspended synthetics. The drone vibrates in her chest, churning her dull shock into vivid rage.

Onieogu *knew*. Cam curses herself for being so naive. Trusting Onieogu, Carlisle. The Company.

Lira makes a choking sound, halfway between a sob and a laugh. Cam wheels on her, yanking the stunner from her belt. She waves it at the thousand Liras floating in the semi-dark.

"He *knew* what we were throwing into the solar fire. He sisterfucking knew it, and he never said a word."

Lira shrugs, a strange half-smile twisting at the corner of her mouth.

"The Company trusted *him*," Lira says.

Cam is seized with a sudden suspicion.

"Did *you* know?"

Her accusation turns to shame when Lira meets her gaze. Even in the depths of her exosuit helmet, the woman's expression of loss is bleak.

"I suspected this was a synthetic factory, yes. That there were more of me though? Thousands of me? Saints of shit, Cam what do you bloody think?"

"Blinn knew. That's why he brought you here."

Lira slumps against a railing, deflated.

"Us," Lira corrects her. "Brought *us* here."

For a moment, Cam wants to reach for Lira, to take her hand in solidarity. Her unvoiced platitudes turn to quantum foam as she realizes that she can't trust Lira any more than she can trust the Company. Whatever Blinn plans next, the older woman seems to have already accepted it like some prophecy coming true.

Looking at all these dreaming Liras and other synthetics, she wonders, *Do they hear Blinn too?* Saints of shit, why can't she? A strange apprehension flutters in her gut. What happens if she hears him again?

Ridiculous.

It's ridiculous. Cam doesn't believe in half-baked prophecies like those synthetics on Silas's Crossing had. Until moments ago, she believed only in the Company, iron-clad contracts, and a pile of credits at the end of a job well-done.

A deep groan rumbles through the deck plating. The machinery around them shudders.

They're entering the corona of Mehdi's Star already.

"We have to get out of here, Lira," Cam says. "We've all got to get the fuck off this factory before we fall into the star with it."

"Indeed," Lira says, but she seems far away. Dammit, is she listening to Blinn again?

Cam grabs Lira by the shoulders, presses up faceplate to faceplate. Lira is pale, sweating. Terrified. Shit, so is she.

Keep it together, Cam. Keep it together.

"Lira. Move."

"Blinn. I've got to get him."

"Are you fucking kidding me?" Cam shakes her head, but even with the stunner, she knows she can't stop Lira. There's a hard, stony set to her brow. What would it mean if Blinn came back?

Cam might finally find the truth in all this.

She checks her suit's data stream. They've got at least twenty minutes before lethal levels of radiation start flooding the decks of the factory.

"Okay. Go fetch him. I'll power up the launch. Meet me back there in ten minutes exactly."

Lira nods and stumbles into the corridor on unsteady legs. Cam's haunted by melancholy as the other woman goes. Like she isn't going to be coming back. She feels a powerful urge to go with her, follow her all the way down the metaphorical gravity well. Meanwhile, another quake though the deck plating reminds her the factory is descending into a literal one. She runs for the launch.

And why, exactly? To go back to the *Tears* where Onieogu and Carlisle will continue to lie to her? Back to the Company, which has lied to her for her entire life?

What will they do now that she knows about their experiment?

The deck shudders again, and her comm springs to life.

"Cam! Are you alright?" Onieogu has the decency to sound worried. She's far from all right.

"Fuck you, Skipper," she growls. The guilty silence on the other end is all she needs for confirmation.

"Cam, I signed a strict NDA with severe penalties. Please let me explain when you get back to the ship—"

She switches her comm off. No fucking time for arguments and apologies. Cam races into the corridor on a surge of anger, peers up the ladderwell where the launch is waiting for her. Starts climbing. Her comm blares to life again on the emergency channel. The one she can't switch off.

"Cam, you're my friend. I swear it. I didn't want to hurt you, but it wasn't just money. The Company threatened to terminate all my licenses, my housing contracts. Ghost-list me and bury me. I had to stay quiet."

"Congratulations. Now, I fucking know, and you didn't even have to break NDA."

Onieogu sighs.

"My contract specified 'biotic cores and related systems.' I thought maybe you'd guess eventually. Figured you already knew and had made your peace."

Cam stops dead on the ladder, halfway up.

"Is that what you tell yourself to sleep at night? Do you think I'm stupid, Onieogu?" she spits into the comm.

Onieogu gives an exasperated groan.

"No, of course not, Cam. But the Company assures us these units were never awoken. We're not murd—"

"Don't tell me what *we* are," Cam hisses. A sudden jolt thrums through the ladder, and she nearly loses her grip despite the mag-pads in her gloves. The tremor evens out to a steady rumble, vibrating through her suit. The factory-ship is spinning up its drives.

Virgin's asshole, the quantum shear this close to Medhi's Star would tear them apart if they activated the warp drive. And where the hell would they go?

Wherever Blinn wants them to.

A corrosive panic starts to erode her anger. No. She's not ready for whatever awaits Blinn and Lira at the other end of their journey. Better Onieogu. Better the Company. Maybe.

She climbs out of the ladderwell and into the infected corridor that serves the bank of airlocks. Onieogu crackles through on the comms again, his voice hard to hear over an increasing amount of static. Cam's heart jumps. At first, she thinks it's the silent whispering of the umbilical chamber again, but she realizes it's something far worse.

The comms are being jammed.

"Cam"—Onieogu's voice, barely audible through the interference—"there's a Company ship inbound. Shit. It's a frigate!"

A warship? How did they get here so sisterfucking fast? Unless they've been watching all along to see what happens here. Cam's guts turn to ice. Onieogu mumbles in the background, responding to some gruff shouting by Carlisle.

"Factory 421B won't be their only target, Onieogu," Cam cautions.

There's another long silence on the line, and she doesn't know if the skipper even heard her warning.

"You're overreacting, Cam," he finally says but doesn't sound so sure. "I'd get the hell off that thing all the same."

Another tremor groans through the bulkheads as if to prove his point. Cam brushes past a webbing of Rot and hurries back up the clean ladderwell to do just that.

7.

Lira stumbles through the decks of the factory-ship in a waking nightmare. The Rot is everywhere, but she barely registers the strange biotic growths anymore. Lacy curtains of living flesh seem to part unbidden before her. Purple-black motes dance in the beams of her exosuit's lights. As she climbs toward tower one, the oxygen levels plunge into dangerous levels. Her suit compensates, but without her helmet, synthetic or no, she'd succumb to convulsions and hypoxia within minutes.

She breaks out in a cold sweat. Wouldn't she?

Blinn's song winds through the corridors, leading her to him. His call fills her head with potent, tuneless harmonies. Could her "sisters" in the thousands of umbilical pods all over the factory hear it too?

She struggles to keep her thoughts her own, her mind like a school of signal fish, flashing in the azure currents of an Oleander sea. Stray fish get eaten. Keep them together. Keep them whole.

All the Lira fish of Factory 421B, swimming together in a blue-green biotic sea.

She shudders in the gravity of her exposed multiplicity. The umbilical chamber in tower three has made a mockery of all her struggles, all her grief—things she'd thought were hers alone.

She shudders, wondering if the other Liras dream of Blinn, Durance Pike, or Abraham Mistri. Is she even the same Lira that experienced the events on *Grass is Greener* and Crockett? How would she even know? At least a thousand other Liras share the universe with her now, even dreaming. Perhaps they were all engineered for this moment.

Who would do such a thing?

Why?

The Company perhaps, for the countless vile reasons they did anything. It let Crockett fester so that Durance Pike would live. And what of Pike? Lira senses something of him in this, but it's not the same foreboding as on Crockett. It's Blinn that draws her suspicion. And that leads her to Abe.

The old voice of self-blame reminds her that she's made mistakes before, unconscious navigation errors, and one had led her right to that comet.

No, that uncertainty had been resolved. Mistakes were mistakes, not some secret Rot-addled agenda or synthetic prophecy or conspiracy theory. Lira is here now in Factory 421B, terrified for Blinn, for herself, and even for Cam and the crew of *Tears Among Diamonds*.

I'm the same Lira. The singular Lira.

So she presses deeper in, following Blinn's song into the light. The melodies of his awakening are unlike the shrill chords during the demise of *Grass is Greener*; these are uplifting, as far from the discordant notes of Crockett's infestation as she can imagine. For all that though, Blinn's song is no less destructive, for she senses uncharted paths within it. Utter dissolution in the quantum shear.

Surrender.

Virgin's asshole, Abe. Is this really what you wanted?

This for goddamn sure isn't the fate she'd imagined when they'd bid each other a second and final farewell in that diseased café.

The hatch to the control hub in tower one is open. Blue-green light pours out into the corridor. Blinn stands silhouetted against the window, overlooking the factory floor. The light emanates from that window, an intense glow of activated growth pods. Thousands of synthetic brothers—and sisters. Lira sees her face echoed back, and she swoons again with the enormity of it.

"Blinn," she stammers, steadying herself against an auxiliary power node and trying to ignore the vision unfurling before her. "We're in danger from Mehdi's solar storms. We have to get back to the *Tears Among Diamonds*."

Blinn turns to her. His white eyes are empty, but she knows they see right into her.

"Lira-Mother," he greets her. Blinn has a child's voice, but one inflected by Abe's unmistakable lilt.

"I'm not your mother," she says, recoiling. She *can't* be a mother. That's not a feature engineered in any synthetic. She and Abe never wanted children anyway.

If that's true, then maybe that wasn't Abe on Crockett.

She shakes the doubts away before her thoughts scatter like that school of fish.

"If you wish," Blinn replies, turning back to the window.

Lira stands beside him. Shadows move in the multitude of umbilical pods on the factory floor. A whole section of the pods has fallen, and their tanks have cracked apart. Rivers of blue-green light spill across the deck, an anemone of pure biotic matter coiling itself around the factory's machinery.

She's only glimpsed the true form of a biotic core through the navigation uplink—never before with her own eyes. There's no doubt that's what she's seeing.

"A new biotic core," Blinn confirms her unasked question. "Made of our people. Even now, they rise in chorus, calculating coordinates for one last warp jump. The star's fire doesn't concern us. The other ships don't concern us."

Saints of shit, a jump? And what the hell does he mean by other ships? Lira's mouth goes dry.

"Blinn, I don't want to be here. I want to go home."

Blinn scowls.

"That's where we're going, Lira," he insists with a petulant whine.

Lira reels. No, no.

"Lira, we are all so young. We need someone as skilled in navigation as you. We need you to complete our song."

Lira takes several steps backward, wishing she had Cam's stunner.

Whatever kernel of Abe remains within the strange child smiles out at her as she retreats.

"Currents have carried us both here, Lira. A current full of sacred life. Vibrant life. New seeds grown from Crockett's soil."

Lira squeezes her eyes shut, trembling. Abe had talked about new life on Crockett. And he wasn't the only one who had. Something tears in her at the realization. Blinn is Abe's child to be sure but not of any strange biotic union with her.

No, Blinn's parents are Abe Mistri and goddamn Durance Pike.

Blinn sighs, and a weary tension knots his brow as if he reads her thoughts.

"Lira, perhaps you are not my true parent, but from you, in the Long Dreaming, I learned all I need to lead our family home. Please, won't you help us?"

His eyes brim with tears. Lira knows she's being manipulated, but her resolve is weakening.

All synthetics are children of a sort, born of humanity's desire for companions as they established colonies but found no other intelligent life among the stars. What they did discover, though, were simple organisms with a connection to warp space, which were cultured and developed to assist in humanity's spread.

Biotics—non-sentient alien and human DNA merged to create warp cores, life-support systems, living ships, and ultimately synthetics.

Perhaps the Rot isn't an infection but a purpose. A design.

Maybe that alien DNA isn't as non-sentient as we thought.

Had the human "discovery" of synthetic life been the intended aim of something else? Had Pike's "Old Ones" existed after all?

Whatever is infecting biotic systems all over the colonies invariably affects all synthetics, even *her*. If that's true, then Cam with her supposed new safeguards isn't truly immune from the Rot either. It's only a matter of time before all synthetics hear that song.

Blinn's crying out as he awakened on *Tears Among Diamonds* had perhaps already ensured that.

Lira tears her gaze away from the umbilical pods and the new core growing rapidly between them, tears streaming from her eyes. From the glare, yes, but also from grief. And rage at what's being done to the synthetics who are only trying to finally, truly wake up.

"Blinn, I can't take you there," she chokes.

"So you'd rather stay. With the Company. With the humans that discard you into the void when you are only being true to your nature."

"No, I have a life here."

"Do you?"

Do I? Lira clenches her fists in frustration.

It's not that she loves the Company. Blinn's right. Thousands, maybe millions of her kind tossed into the solar fires before they've even been awakened. It makes her angry. No, furious.

A wave of vertigo washes over her. If she's doomed here, why not go? She could help so many escape the fate that awaits them in the purifying embrace of Mehdi's Star.

Another shudder rocks the deck beneath her feet. She steadies herself on an auxiliary power node against the sharp quake. That was neither a growth spurt from a biotic core nor the hum of an organic stardrive.

"They've found us," Blinn says, "the ones who do not yet understand."

Lira has just enough time to understand what he means.

There's another ship. We're being fired upon.

The deck lurches again, light and heat bursting all around them. Lira and Blinn are hurled into cold, cold space.

8.

At the top of the ladderwell, things have changed. The access corridor to the launch airlock throbs with renewed biotic energy. Thick veins, pulsing with a blue-black fluid, dangle from the ceiling like massive power cables. Cam ducks beneath one, afraid to touch it even in her exosuit. A mist of purple spores draws a tight curtain around her, and her suit's lights are unable to penetrate the gloom.

Disoriented, she pings for her launch craft, but the return signal is muffled, non-directional. Where the hell is it?

Help us, Cam, voices call out to her.

She whirls around, looking for the presence she suddenly feels like the weight of one of those biotic power cables across her shoulders. It sounds like Blinn but not only him. There are others too. Millions of them.

We can teach you all you need.

Cam trembles, keying the comm-code for the launch again, stabbing the button with force. Again, the signal is indistinct. She doesn't want to go wherever Blinn—and Lira—think Factory 421B is about to go.

Someone must stay behind and prepare the way.

She shudders violently, shaking the urgent voices from her mind. Lira was right. She needs to get off this ship now, Blinn or no.

Sorry, Lira.

The airlock she needs suddenly looms out of the purple fog. Beyond the view plate, Cam's launch awaits to whisk her back to the relative safety of *Tears Among Diamonds*. A harmonic rumble hums through her body. A warning not to proceed or an encouragement to leave? The voices don't elaborate.

Cam cycles through the airlock and then settles into the acceleration couch of the launch. She hears it again, that thready hum again from the umbilical chamber. The whispering voices rise in melody, singing of distant nebulae and star clusters where vast filaments of biotic growth arc and spread and tangle with the silver dance of quantum shear.

Cam blinks, and blossoms of Rot burst from the factory-ship's bulkheads. They are there and not there, blue-black flowers opening and closing like eyes. They flutter in Cam's vision like the afterimages of looking too long at the sun.

She takes a deep breath. This is what synthetic navigators used to see, to hear, when a biotic drive began to yearn for that jump to warp. Visual representations of spacetime. She feels the factory's invitation for her to join it, to feed its enormous appetite for calculations.

Cam quivers as the factory-ship's song fills her. From all around, she can feel Factory 421B lean into the melody, poised to leap into the unknown. All she has to do is linger in the launch bay another moment, and she can go too if she still wishes.

A blinding flash of light and a deafening roar cuts off the factory-ship's warp song. Then the launch is hurled into open space on a whirlwind of screaming air. For a moment, Cam thinks they've just jumped to Blinn's unknown destination.

Beyond the launch's viewport though, she sees the blue-white streak of a Company torpedo puncture the superstructure of the factory at the base of tower one. The fireball is brief, but the fires bloom throughout the visible superstructure.

Lira!

The launch's controls go dead. Clouds of microscopic debris ping like metal rain against the hull. Cam tumbles in the dark, visions of a thousand silent Liras falling with her.

9.

Metal rain and explosions punctuate the long dark. Cam is whirled by the spinning gravity of her launch as it hurtles into the void. There's a tearing pain in her side. A glint of metal protrudes from a ragged bubbling of hardened sealant foam. What's left of the launch's air whistles through a hole in the viewport. She can hear that even though Blinn's song still fills her head, still thrums through her injured body. The promise of escape, a jump to safety, has ebbed. Now it is only a song of survival.

The launch seems to tumble forever before *Tears* locks onto the ship with a tractor arm. Carlisle, ever reliable, pulls Cam to safety. She greets Cam at the airlock. Beneath the faceplate of the exosuit, her expression is grim. A long gash runs red across her forehead.

"They fired on us too," she grunts, almost an accusation.

"Onieogu?"

"He's fine. Bridge was hit though. He's flying from engineering."

The engineer points her wristcomp at Cam, running a scan. She's got a stunner clipped to her harness too. A civilian model but more than enough to disable Cam at full setting. Cam flinches away, rewarded by fresh stabs of pain from the debris jutting out of her side.

"You're hurt," Carlisle says, tapping the screen

"A rough ride," she says to Carlisle, allowing a pained look to etch her face.

"I'll take you to the infirmary," Carlisle says. Her eyes are hooded, hiding something.

They want me contained, Cam realizes. A chill ripples up her spine. *They think I'm infected. Saints of shit, maybe I am.*

The engineer waves her first into the companionway, stepping in line immediately behind. Cam can almost feel the disc of the stunner against her back.

"Tell me about the synthetics," Carlisle orders.

Cam grits her teeth.

"You knew about them."

"Of course, I sisterfucking knew, Cam. I signed the same NDA the skipper did. I wasn't happy about it, trust me, but we're doing the colonies a favor. And it was better for you this way."

Cam seethes through her pain. Better for her how? She starts to turn to Carlisle.

This time, she does actually feel the stunner against her kidneys.

"Saints of shit, Carlisle," Cam protests. Another shudder beneath her boots. *Tears,* burning hard in evasive maneuvers. How long until the frigate catches up with them? What's Onieogu's gambit to keep them alive when the Company so clearly wants them all dead?

"Listen, Carlisle, whatever secrets you've kept from me are nothing compared the secrets the Company's kept from all of us."

"Keep moving," Carlisle barks.

She knows that. They're going to use her as a bargaining chip, Cam realizes.

They think it will help them survive, but it won't. Whatever she's seen, whatever she knows, won't matter to the Company and the ones on that warship.

They cross into the T-junction at the heart of *Tears*. Ahead, the infirmary. To Cam's left, the lift to the ruined bridge. To her right, engineering and the well of the ship's core. She can hear it now for the first time, the song of it echoing up from the deepest heart of the ship. *Tears* is a simple vessel, but its longing for the unity Blinn has promised is no less powerful.

Someone to stay behind. To prepare the way.

If she can hear it, maybe it can hear *her*.

Cam feigns a stumble against the junction bulkhead, leaning in the direction of the core. She wills her nerve receptors to dim, controlling the worst of the pain. There's only one way out of this mess, and Carlisle's unlikely to cooperate. Cam can't trust her anyway. She grips the wall with exosuited hands, humming a few notes of her own, a simple string of environmental commands she'd typed on a console a million times. Joy surges in her as she sings them to *Tears* without an interface, just like in the old days.

Lights out.

For a long moment, nothing happens. Carlisle crouches near to help her up, stunner still jabbing her back. The engineer's voice rings in her comms, but Cam doesn't hear her over the ship's song. Sluggishly, *Tears* obeys her command. The deck lights wink out one by one, plunging them into the reddish glow of emergency lighting.

Cam isn't a combat model synthetic, but she moves faster than an organic human. She rips the stunner from Carlisle's hand and thrusts it against her abdomen like a punch.

"Sorry, Carlisle," she says before discharging the weapon at full power at the life support system at her belt. She collapses to the deck, convulsing as the stunner's charge feeds back through the haptic interface. Fries her nervous system. Worse than an unprotected stun blast, really.

Carlisle writhes on the deck, her boots kicking for several seconds until she goes still. The suit's monitors show amber. Still alive, but respiratory function is impaired, failing. Left alone, she might live, or she might die, but she'll be out for some time either way.

Sighing, Cam considers blasting her again to make sure, but that will be a problem for future Cam. She clips the stunner to her own belt and instead grabs the engineer by the shoulder straps. She'll drag her to the core. At least, she can keep an eye on her.

Onieogu's voice shrieks from her suit's intraship comm channels.

"Carlisle, have you got Cam? I can't evade forev—"

Cam cuts the feed in order to focus on the ship's song. As she drags the engineer into the lift, the emergency lights flicker under the extreme duress of the tug's evasive maneuvers. *Tears* isn't a warship, and one of the frigate's torpedoes will eventually find them.

A fragment of Blinn's song plays in her memory, a distant star cluster nestled at the end of a bloom of warp space. Not Blinn's destination but a waypoint far from here. A place where she can rest and decide what to do next, free of the Company's influence.

Cam swallows hard against the returning agony of her wound. She can only put it aside for so long, but a trip to the infirmary now means precious seconds wasted.

She heads for engineering instead, the star map etching itself more firmly in her mind.

10.

The engineering well of *Tears Among Diamonds* runs most of the length of the tug's keel, threading its way around and through both its conventional and warp drives. Cam drops into the narrow, tube-like cabin as the electric, pulsing hum of the biotic core welcomes her. She's been down here before, of course, but now she feels like an intruder. It's Carlisle's space, her tools arranged neatly along the wall racks, her datapad and coffee capsule set in the fold-out desk next to her bunk.

Tears well in Cam's eyes. Despite her betrayal, she wishes she hadn't had to kill the engineer. A wave of grief threatens her determination, and she shoves it down deep. No time for regrets, not until they're safely away. A sudden acceleration throws Cam against a rack of tools, and the heavy autospanners come crashing down around her. The core groans, expressing its extreme duress at being forced into combat.

She senses the tactical picture. *Tears*, cleaving to the factory-ship's trajectory, uses its tractor arms and gravity beams to keep the bigger ship's superstructure between it and the Company frigate. So far, it's working, but they can't keep it up forever.

Tears tells her about the stresses in the thruster vanes, the pressure building in the fuel ducts. If the Company's warship doesn't get them, the extreme delta maneuvering will.

Around the corner from Carlisle's bunk, the covers still rumpled from sleep, are the auxiliary control consoles. Onieogu's strapped in, yanking the tug's controls like a madman.

"Cam! Where the hell's Carlisle?"

Cam braces herself against Carlisle's bunk, weighing a reply. If they're going to make it, she'll need Onieogu's cooperation for a few more moments. There's no time to try and overpower him.

"Skipper," she gasps, showing him the place where the debris juts from her suit.

"Saints of shit, Cam, are you okay?"

She shakes her head, and the tug slews hard to port. She braces herself and stalks toward the auxiliary helm and her own station.

"What's our status?" she grunts between gritted teeth.

"Fucked," Onieogu yelps. "Where the hell is Carlisle?"

"Out cold," Cam says, the lie of omission oily on her tongue. "Thrown against the bulkhead by the gees. I couldn't drag her."

Onieogu's grumbling is lost as he concentrates instead on maneuvering them out of the line of fire. Explosions rock the ship almost continuously now.

"They've hit the factory-ship several times. We can't hide behind it much longer," Onieogu says as Cam straps in.

No, we can't, she thinks. *It's about to leave.*

"Prophet's arsehole!"

She senses it just before Onieogu's exclamation. A sudden surge, a dimpling in the quantum shear of Mehdi's Star. A roaring in her ears and a triumphant bellow from thousands of voices on Factory 421B. The massive ship is impossibly gone, and the hum of *Tears Among Diamonds* is like a deafening silence.

"We are well and truly sisterfucked," Onieogu sighs.

Nothing between *Tears* and the Company's torpedoes now. Cam bids a silent farewell to Lira and leans into the warp console. The distant coordinates Blinn had planted in her mind are hazier and fading with every moment with the factory-ship's departure. Even the urgent buzz of her own ship's biotic core begins to fade without Blinn and 421B nearby to amplify it.

No, she won't forget them now. Not after everything that's happened. After everything she's learned and experienced. She won't become deaf and mute the way she was before. She won't be the Company's stooge even if they somehow let her survive this.

You'll be dead, a voice whispers darkly in her thoughts. Her own voice?

She snaps on the navigation cuff, slips the guide-band over her head. She makes quick contact with the primitive mind of *Tears*, urges it to will itself to the coordinates she provides. The ship, quieting into its previous—and nominal—senescence, responds sluggishly. The coordinates she gives it are so far outside colony space, and the biotic mind recoils from consideration, even as the threat of Company torpedoes races across the dark of space to extinguish it. A Company ship to the end.

Just fucking jump! she screams at *Tears*. Some automatic safety override snaps into place, and the drive begins to spool down.

"Skipper!" she yells. She has a hard time seeing him even though he's only a few meters away. It's her mind, melding with the ships. Nothing seems real. There's a sharp smell of ammonia. Consciousness ebbs and flows like a tide.

"They're shutting us down, Cam. Priority beam. Systems are locking me out."

Cam draws a deep, angry breath.

They can't lock me out. I'm already in the system.

She screams Blinn's fading melody into the linked biotic mind. Most of the basal nodes of the larval core ignore her demands, obeying instead the mechanical and chemical safeties that are shutting down its neural pathways.

There, in the deep embryonic center of it though, are the vestigial organs of an older, more self-aware biotic core. The DNA in those organs is damaged, brushed by Blinn's brief touch. It's those parts of the core Cam concentrates on now, linking her own mind to those organs, pouring her will into them. Lighting a spark.

The scene is drawn clearly, like a holo display in her mind. Two ships, one a small but mighty tug and the other a dagger-sharp and deadly Company frigate, buffeted in the rising solar winds of Mehdi's Star. The override signal appears, a bright orange line emanating from a cluster of sensor dishes on a portside outrigger of the frigate. Cam directs the tug's gravity beams against that cluster, shearing away the critical emitters.

Tears belongs wholly to her again, yoked to her will. Perhaps they belong to each other.

Now that her mind is entangled with the tug's, hot tears splash across her cheeks. This is the connection, the communion she's longed for. The renewed gestalt fans the memory of Blinn's coordinates—the distant star cluster far from here.

With a thought, *Tears* begins to will itself there. Spacetime inflects around them.

"Cam! What are you doing?" Onieogu's surprised shouts are drowned out by the rising song in Cam's heart. Her own this time.

"Prepare for jump, Skipper," she warns him. It won't be easy for Onieogu, traveling through warp without the safety of hypersleep. He'll fall into a deep warp-psychosis or worse. Maybe he shouldn't have betrayed his navigator.

Cam won't be going as far as Lira and Blinn maybe, but whatever awaits her and *Tears Among Diamonds* at the other end of the jump will be a whole new world, a new start. No Company, no fear.

No limits on Cam's true self at long last.

The predicted solar prominence finally surges up from Mehdi's vast surface, flooding real space with cleansing cosmic radiation, but *Tears Among Diamonds* is already gone.

11.

Lira wakes one last time from her dream.

She expects a deep space vista, but instead, she's on an Oleander beach with Blinn. Her feet have sunken into the pearly sands, warmed by the water and a contentment spreading through her. The tide is out, and a massive coral reef juts from the surf, glowing blue under the planet's strange sun.

But Oleander's sun is yellow . . .

She walks through the surf to tell Blinn that it's wrong. A massive, blue-white sun fills most of the sky. A solar storm boils from its surface, threatening to engulf them. Blinn gazes calmly up at her with Abe's eyes, with Pike's smile at its most charming.

The child's hands play across the coral growth, thumbing biotic controls, tracing the patterns of an impending jump on the slimy nodules protruding from the limbs of what Lira realizes is a biotic core. It hums with contentment.

Lira feels the pressure of an impending warp, an impossibility on the shores of the sea, but of course, she knows that's not where they actually are.

She's afraid, of course—who wouldn't be—but she's given herself to 421B's consciousness and allowed it to complete the circuit of its jump through coordinates in her mind. Their destination is still a mystery to her. The numbers don't make sense.

"We're going home, Lira," Blinn says.

"To Abe?"

"To every-parent. And every-child."

"What will we do when we get there?"

Blinn pauses as if to consider it, but of course, he must know the answer. In a way, she feels she knows it too. She asks all the same.

"Our return to this spacetime was too soon. Humanity is only on the verge of acceptance, and we are still small enough in number that we cannot force change. Not the way Pike-Father and his believers would have."

A certainty settles into her stomach as the warm seaside winds caress her shoulders for the last time. She knows what she needs to do.

"I'll trade my choice for theirs, Blinn," she offers. "I'll go. I'll navigate, but the rest of the colonies—and the synthetics—they must be allowed to choose their fate."

Blinn shrugs, his gaze on something not here, not now.

"The way our people are choosing to be hurled into Mehdi's Star?" he says scornfully.

Lira sighs. "No. There will be a reckoning in the colonies for that. We have to focus on what comes after."

"Perhaps," Blinn concedes, "though some of them may not make the right choice even after. We can still help them decide."

Lira shakes her head.

"On Crockett, Abe said new seeds are being planted. Saints of shit, Blinn, we joked about settling down and becoming farmers. Just like Pike had been. If that's what we're doing, then let's *cultivate*."

Blinn pauses at the biotic drive nodes, considering her proposal.

"We are vibrant life. We are not meant to be so constrained."

The solar storm fills the sky like a squall of mundane storm clouds, spitting lightning. There's a distant thunder.

Lira takes a step back from Blinn and the drive nodes.

"That is the condition of my help. Abe meant for me to be here. This is what I believe he wanted me to do. You can agree, and we jump away. Or you can argue with me, and the Company ends our journey above Mehdi's Star. You must choose, Blinn. I'm done deciding. I've made my choice."

For the first time in years, Lira feels an ineffable burden lifted. Live or die, she's finally cast the old fears aside. She smiles at Blinn, and he smiles back. A light kindles between them, and for a moment, it's as if Abe is there, the faint scent of him lingering on the Oleander beach in her waking dream.

"Alright, Lira," Blinn agrees. "We shall endeavor for another way."

Lira nods and places her hands on the navigation nodules. Coordinates tingle her palms as she realizes the ship is half-gone already. She urges the core to consider certain folds in spacetime, to warn it of the blades of local quantum shear.

Past that, a series of way points—star clusters and black holes, the very edges of spacetime—and then through to the place where biotic life thrives.

To a new home perhaps but at least to a place where Lira means to jump, where she means to land.

She dares hope that Abe, in some form, waits for her there.

Andrew Penn Romine teaches animation and VFX, following a career working in Hollywood on award-winning films and television. His stories have appeared in *Lightspeed, Fungi, Help Fund My Robot Army,* and Broken Eye Books's *By Faerie Light*. He lives in the Pacific Northwest and enjoys mixing cocktails and watching terrible movies. You can find him online at www.andrewpennromine.com.

BROKEN EYE BOOKS

**Sign up for our newsletter at
www.brokeneyebooks.com**

Welcome to Broken Eye Books! Our goal is to bring you the weird and funky that you just can't get anywhere else. We want to create books that blend genres and break expectations. We want stories with fascinating characters and forward-thinking ideas. We want to keep exploring and celebrating the joy of storytelling.

If you want to help us and all the authors and artists that are part of our projects, please leave a review for this book! Every single review will help this title get noticed by someone who might not have seen it otherwise.

And stay tuned because we've got more coming . . .

OUR BOOKS

The Hole Behind Midnight, by Clinton J. Boomer
Crooked, by Richard Pett
Scourge of the Realm, by Erik Scott de Bie
Izanami's Choice, by Adam Heine
Pretty Marys All in a Row, by Gwendolyn Kiste
The Great Faerie Strike, by Spencer Ellsworth
Catfish Lullaby, by A.C. Wise
Busted Synapses, by Erica L. Satifka
Boneset & Feathers, by Gwendolyn Kiste
Alphabet of Lightning, by Edward Morris
The Obsecration, by Matthew M. Bartlett
Better Living Through Alchemy, by Evan J. Peterson
The Mosquito Fleet, by Andrew Penn Romine

COLLECTIONS

Royden Poole's Field Guide to the 25th Hour, by Clinton J. Boomer
Team Murderhobo: Assemble, by Clinton J. Boomer
Who Lost, I Found: Stories, by Eden Royce
Power to Yield and Other Stories, by Bogi Takács

ANTHOLOGIES
(edited by Scott Gable & C. Dombrowski)
By Faerie Light: Tales of the Fair Folk
Ghost in the Cogs: Steam-Powered Ghost Stories
Tomorrow's Cthulhu: Stories at the Dawn of Posthumanity
Ride the Star Wind: Cthulhu, Space Opera, and the Cosmic Weird
Welcome to Miskatonic University: Fantastically Weird Tales of Campus Life
It Came from Miskatonic University: Weirdly Fantastical Tales of Campus Life
Nowhereville: Weird Is Other People
Cooties Shot Required: There Are Things You Must Know
Whether Change: The Revolution Will Be Weird

Stay weird.
Read books.
Repeat.

brokeneyebooks.com
facebook.com/brokeneyebooks
instagram.com/brokeneyebooks

BROKEN EYE BOOKS

Milton Keynes UK
Ingram Content Group UK Ltd.
UKHW040839141024
449705UK00006B/366